Detective Joan Coleman series

2

mia mornar

Published by mia mornar, 2023.

DETECTIVE JOAN COLEMAN SERIES

First edition. March 21, 2023.

ISBN: 979-8215578681

Written by mia mornar.

Anne was sitting on her balcony holding a glass of wine in her hands on her 12-floor apartment on 22nd Street Avenue in San Francisco. She was waiting for her boyfriend Daniel to show up.

It was already late.' She could hear a terrible noise: some couple had been having an argument down the street.. 'She was thinking' Daniel will show up or not!?'

'She and Daniel meet each other on the filming set. They fall in love soon after."

It has been 2 years since she met Daniel. Anne is pretty in a flawed accessible way. Her eyes peered out through a wild tangle of hair like those of a cornered animal. Her gray-blue eyes make her such an irresistible woman. Her voice is low and chilling. Blonde, somewhat fragile, intelligent in expression. Her skin is very soft and pale but so beautiful. The night was cold. She stood up to put the jumper on, she went to the toilet to refresh her face, she felt so tired after all day shooting the new movie. Getting to the kitchen she starts to feel very hungry. She took the first pan, two eggs and the last slice of bread hanging down the bottom of the cupboard. She didn't have time to do some shopping lately. Feeling chilly in her body didn't want to wait anymore for him to show up so she finally lay down in her bed. It was a big day ahead!'

Around 2 pm in the morning, something wakes her up. She had Tommy cat with her sitting cozy close to her. She moves the cat from the bed and studs up to check what was that noise.'?

Walking very slowly around the apartment Anne couldn't see anyone. It was dark but that noise was coming from the living room. Approaching the kitchen and the toilet without making any noise someone grabs her from behind.! 'She screams!.' He puts his hand on her lips and whispers in her ears.'

Hi, my darling It's me, Daniel. He touches her breast very softly. his hands were moving lower and lower. She felt very excited. Oh, Daniel, she turns around to kiss him barely saying anything. He wanted her so badly. He heard her sigh as their bodies filled each other's skin, its coolness turning to heat... Anne felt very happy to see Daniel after a couple of weeks of being apart. He was working on the new film the same as she did. She gets up having a quick shower, kisses Daniel saying:" Darling I got to go to work. Can you meet later at 'Lazy Bear' to have a nice meal! How about 8 pm? 'She asked.'

Daniel was half asleep but he could hear what she was suggesting. He turns towards her holding her hand, smiling happily. He added' yes no problem I will be at Lazy Bear.' love you, Anne.!'

'She had a busy day ahead.'

Later that day Anne took the cab to the 'Lazy Bear restaurant. She was on time.

She orders a glass of wine waiting for Daniel. She's been sitting there for 2 hours but Daniel didn't come. She was trying to call him on the mobile phone but there was no answer.

She was feeling very tired of waiting so she decided to go back home. She was thinking:' Oh probably he didn't hear me at all this morning but he didn't even answer the phone, that was strange.!'

Arriving at home, a little cat was sitting on her bed. Daniel wasn't there. On the kitchen table was a little note left.'

'Dear Anne.' It was great last night. Something came up. I will not be able to meet you tonight.

Hope you had a great day today!. I will call you later today! Love Daniel.'

She was standing there staring at the message he had left. She stretches her hair thinking; what the hell!' Where is he?' why did he leave so suddenly.?'

She felt very exhausted after working all day. Somehow this weird behavior from Daniel was driving her crazy at the point she didn't know what to think about this relationship anymore. Her life was perfect, a great satisfying job, good friends, nice apartment, only her love life was on the edge.' Anne's parents have died a long time ago, the disappearance of her old sister happened a long time ago. Nobody knew that she had a sister. Anne wanted to find her!'

'She put hot water running to have a nice hot bath later that night.

Preparing to go to bed she took a book from the shelf to read before her late sleep.

During that night, someone broke into Anne's apartment around 3 pm in the morning.

The strange footsteps were getting closer to Anne's room.

He was inside the room. He could see she was sleeping. He pulls Annie for the legs, putting his hands on her mouth to shut her up.

Her frightened eyes went round and round the ring of faces. He was dressed all in black she could see. Very tall guy, his eyes were brown and deep, somehow scary. The rest of his face she couldn't see, the mask was covering the rest of his face. Anne was terrified. In her mind, she wanted to live! She wanted to see Daniel once again.

She was trying to fight him back while he was dragging her to the balcony she screamed, it was too late he pushed her from the 12 floors. Next morning she was in the newspaper.

'The famous actress Anne Wilson is dead.'

'San Francisco police department.'

Police received a phone call around 4.30pm in the morning about Anne Willson.

Detective Carl was in charge of this murder.

'What the hell's been going on ?' the first asked, staring down at Michael.

"We have another murder," said Michael.'

'Let's go.' Carl said.'

'Let me get something on.' said Michael.

Some neighbors have called for Anne Wilson is murdered.' said Michael.'

Carl asked.' Did he say his name?

Michael added:' 'He's an old man. I believe his name is Chris.'

'Okay, let's go then.' said Michael.'

'Detectives left the police station driving to the crime scene.' It was coming at 5 pm in the morning.' The dead body of Anne Wilson was standing there in the middle of the street covered in blood.'

"The first came out from the car detective Carl.' He was holding his gun in his left hand.'

He was observing the dead body of Anne Willson. He knew she was pushed down from her Apartment. There was blood everywhere.'

'Hey Carl, I think this must be Mr Chriss, he heard most of the thing from his window.' said Maichel.'

'Detective Carl replied.' Oh, that's good. After we finish with Mr Chris we are going to check Apartment of Miss Anne.' There seemed to be some disgust in his tone as he pointed down at the dead women lying on the floor.'

'The group of Forensic came just on time.'

'Mr Criss came, he was an old man in his 70's.' His legs were barely moving, too old I guess.'

Detective Carl asked:' you must be Mr Chriss?'

Chris looked at him pointing with his finger at the dead body:' I heard the noise, then screamed.

I couldn't see the figure of the men or women or whoever did this horrible thing to this girl. She was a very nice girl. 'The old man carries on talking.' I knew she had a boyfriend Daniel, I believe he was an actor as well.'

'Detective Carl was listening very carefully to every single word.' Then asked.'

'Did anyone maybe get out the back way?'

'The old man scratches his eyebrow.' said:

' No I haven't seen anyone but as I said I did hear very well the noise then women scream.'

I'm sorry I can't help you more.

Detective Carl pushed his hand into his right pocket like he was looking for something. He appeared to be very nervous.' Said;' Thank you, Mr Chris.' And of course, one more thing if you remember anything please call us.'

'Detective Michael said: Come on Carl, are you finished with the old man!?' He was scratching his head, he seemed to be very irritated.'

'There is work to do, there is still Apartment to check!!' Let's go!!'

Detective Carl replies:' Yes I know! you go. I will be with you in a couple of minutes. We have to find her boyfriend Daniel.' said: Carl.'

I believe he is the key'.

Murmured to himself.' Another crazy murder! I got to call my friend 'Detective John Coleman, he is very good at resolving murders like this.'

'Detective Carl took the stairs to the 12th floor. He was hoping to find out something, he believed that the killer used the stairs after he killed Anne.' Nothing unusual has happened. Reaching the Apartment Michael was already there doing his job..' Carl has found the note of her boyfriend Daniel.'

'Nothing we can do at the moment.' Said Carl!'

I just found this note on the kitchen table.' We have to look for Daniel.' Carl said:'

Michael's anger was rising again:' We have no choice.'

'Let me see this note.' Michale asked:'

'Reading the note he was realizing they have to act quick!'

Carl added:' This afternoon I will give a call to my old friend Detective John Coleman. He can help us a lot in this investigation.'

'Michael wasn't happy to hear that!'

'He gets close to Carl!' 'What's going on? Michael asked:

'You need another Detective to resolve this murder?'

'He appeared to be very furious after hearing that!'

'Detective Carl said: hey listen, man, this has nothing to do with you or with your job!' I need him around. He is brilliant in resolving mysterious murder like this!'

'You go now Michael, get some rest now!' Carl said:'

'What?? Michael shouted:'

'I'm not going anywhere there is work to do, I don't need a bloody rest!!'

'Who do you think you are talking to?'

His eyebrows stuck together he looked so angry to the point that he couldn't concentrate on the job he was doing.'

'Detective Carl raises his voice'! 'Listen, Michael, You are so impulsive, you are getting too angry. As I said before we need 'John Coleman here. And this has nothing to do with you.'

If you want to stay in this Apartment then stay and do your job.! I have to go back to the Police station.' I think we are done here for today!' Carl went out of the Apartment moving fast to the elevator.'

Michael shouted:' Wait I'm coming.' He closes the door of Anne's Apartment. He runs quickly to catch Carl who was already waiting in the elevator.' Carl was in the rush to reach the Police station.'

Michael said with understanding:' Hey Carl I'm really sorry. You know I have been a little angry I admit but I do understand why you want Detective John Coleman to help us.!'

'This is the hard case and we will do it together as a professional team.' So what do you think?'

'Carl's eyes were smiling as he felt some kind of relief'; 'Thanks, Michael.' Carl added:'

'There we were walking to the car.' Each of them was thinking who was the killer of Anne Wilson?'

'Too much work is in this case, this is just the beginning.' Murmured Carl.'

I Got to find this Daniel !' thought Carl.'

'Arr Arriving at the police station Carl closes the door from his office. He lowers the cups of coffee in his cup and drinks it in one go.' He picks up the phone to call John Coleman.'

'The phone was ringing and ringing.'

'There was a moment's silence then a deep voice appeared from the other line.'

John Coleman said:' hello who is this?'

'Carl was happy to finally hear his old friend's voice like in old times.' he said:' Hey man how are you? It's me, Carl!' Good to hear your voice!' 'Carl was smiling.'

'John has been surprised but happy.' He added: Hey, so good to hear back from you! What's up? John asked.'

'Carl was puffing his cigarette '; He said: I was wondering if you can help us ?! around here we have a homicide. The actress Anne Wilson was murdered this morning around 5 pm. As we know so far she has been pushed from the 12 floors.'

'Carl's face turned into a hot red.'

Hmm murmured John:' he asked:' so far do you have anything, maybe a person who has seen the killer walking out from the Apartment? I mean anything!?'

'Carl has stood up from his cheer holding the phone in one hand.' He said:' Well the old guy by name Chris did hear the noise and scream of the women but he didn't see anyone.' we are looking for her boyfriend Daniel.' he is an actor as well apparently they have been in the relationship for 2 years. That's all that we have so far.' And of course, the forensic team they have done the work.' still waiting for the fingerprints to show up.'

John remained in silence for a couple of seconds then said:' Hm I understand. Well, I'm free at the moment which means I can help you guys to resolve this mysterious murder. You know how we work as you told me already we have to find this Daniel then we will know more. I'm sure.'

'I can come tomorrow in San Francisco so we can start to work on this case!'

Carl laid the paper down on what he was holding in hand.' said: ' that's brilliant!'

'Carl felt very happy .' said: Thanks, man. I really appreciate it... So see you tomorrow. Give me a call before you land so I will come to pick you up at the airport!'

John responds: ' See you tomorrow Carl.'

'Carl has put his phone down, his brain has been active, he was thinking who killed Anne Willson.'!

"It was coming late, he left the office with his arm full of the paperwork and went down the stairs to the floor below to leave the note for Michael.'

' The following morning Carl woke up at 6.30 am. He put on a black suit with his dark brown shoes and went to the kitchen to make the coffee. While he was making breakfast the house phone rang.' He stood up from his kitchen table to answer the phone.' He was already starting to sweat. Carl has a health issue with his heart. He's never married any children, no family left. He was a man in his 50's. He did have plans to retire soon; this job was too stressful for him. Apart from that, he did like his job very much.'

'He walks into the living room to answer the phone. He was watching down the window, the rain was falling you could feel the cold ear blowing thru the gaps of the window.' he answers the phone.'

Hello: how is this? He asked.'

Detective John Coleman was on the line.'

Hi, Carl, It's me:! Said John.'

" There was a pause, then Carl responded.' Hi John. Where are you? He asked;

John, he scratched his eye brown for the moment: he said.' I'm fine. I'm calling you to inform you I will arrive at the airport SFO terminal 3 in about one hour.'

'Carl was silent for a minute or two then he said:' Excellent I will be there.'

John added;' Thanks!'

'The conversation ended:' 'Carl has finished his early breakfast. He took his medication every day ready to go to the airport.'

'Driving fast as he didn't want to be late there was some traffic on the main road as always.'

" He thought to himself:' It's been a long time since I've seen John! I guess he didn't change much as a person.' 'He smiles to himself.'

'Arriving at the airport there was always the same problem to find the parking.' too many bloody cars around!' Driving around Carl finally has found the space to park his car.' He jumps quickly from the car, checking that everything is close and clumpy as always. He hit his leg into a big truck that was standing there next to his little car.'

He squeaks; Auch, damn truck!

'Moving quickly so he can finally see his friend John.'

'He could see John, who was waiting there sitting in the lobby.'

'John is a brilliant detective who often solves difficult cases for the police.he was wearing a black suit and dark sunglasses and always had a cold emotionless expression on his face.

He was scratching his beard holding a big cigar in his left hand waiting to bite. He is a man very close to 55. Never lost any case in his life career. Tall somehow very pale in his face.

Profonde brown eyes and very thick eyebrows following the figure of this man.'

'Carl has thought to himself as he saw him;' Oh It's him, he didn't change much at all.'

'He was getting closer to John. he raised his voice saying:' Hey John Is this really you!? Like in old times.'

John has seen him smiling loudly:' E hehe, yes It's me, man. How are you, it's good to see you Carl.!: Haven't changed much; said John;' He was scratching his beard up and down.'

Carl added;' I'm ok. I have some problems with my heart but the rest is ok.'

'Carl said:' let me help you with your suitcase.' he offered to.'

'There were walking towards the car parking;' John paused and looked around:' he asked:'

What can you tell me about this murder?'

Carl scratched his head for a moment then added:' Uff not much for the moment! As I told you on the phone the girl has been pushed from her balcony we are still working on the fingerprints.but the most important thing, in this case, is to find this Daniel. He left the note on the kitchen table the day Anne was murdered.!'

'John has puffed smoke into the air:' He said:' Hmm, I believe there is a strong motive behind all of this.

What I would suggest is to check the bank statement of Anne Willson, does she have any family?' John has asked;'

'Carl murmured.:' Hm, we didn't check this yet!'

John added:' ok Carl, as soon as I leave my suitcase in the hotel and refresh myself we will start to work. It's very important to collect all information, evidence, witnesses if It's any? He has asked:

Carl said:' yes of course! About the witnesses, I only have got the old man, Mr Chriss. But I already interrogated him. He only heard some noise then screamed that's all.'

John asked:' To begin with, do you suspect one particular person?'

Carl's face went hard:' He takes a deep breath; up!' He replies;' Somehow I do suspect this Daniel.' Strange he left the note on the kitchen table, he didn't show up, he didn't call. He has simply disappeared somewhere!' I wonder if he knows that his girlfriend has been murdered?' 'Carl raises his voice!'

'John tapped him on the shoulder.' he added;' That's why I'm here to help you! Definitely, we do have to find this person as soon as possible and we will !'

'The car has stopped in front of the G San Francisco Hotel.'

'John has quickly collected his suitcase from Carl's car saying:' Ok Carl. I will see you in 2 hours! It's a pleasure to work with you again like in old times, remember!?' John has smiled;'

Carl said:' Thanks, man. It's good to have you here!' Hey, I haven't asked you yet!' How is your family? He asked:

John said:' Oh my family, they are all good, thanks for asking! Saying in deeply voice:'

'Carl has shut the door of the car behind him:'

He added; Ok John . See you in 2 hours. I'm going back to the Police station! I will see you there. Thanks!'

John replied:' Yes in 2 hours!' Bye for now!'

'Carl has come back to the Police Station.' Michael was there sitting in his office waiting for Carl to show up.'

'As soon as he heard Carl's voice he jumped from the chair to approach him.'

'Where the hell have you been?' Asked Michael.'

Carl answered sharply;' I left you a note on your desk! I went to pick up John Coleman from the airport this morning. He will be with us soon!'

Michael thought for a second then said:' Hmm, so he is already here?! He asked:'

'Oh well said Michael:' I can't wait to meet him! I have heard about him, he is a brilliant detective!'

'There was a little bit of arrogance in his voice.'

Carl said:' We have a big case to solve. The next step is to find Daniel!' Did you find something about this man?' Carl asked:'

'Michael murmured:' As a matter of fact I did. His name is Daniel Harper. I find he works on the new film production down the coast in 'San Jose.' I also looked into the Anne accounts. I found an interesting thing. She has not had a family member, she is the only child. Her parents died in a car accident.' And what is interesting is that she had a pile of money in her bank account and some of it is on the Daniel name,' so what do you think boss!?'

'Carl sketch his eyebrow'; you have done an excellent job !! well done Michael!'

So the first thing is to drive to San Jose to find this man;' said Carl, holding one hand in his pocket.!'

'The taxi stopped in front of the Police department it was John Coleman:'

'He was puffing his cigar looking around,' He enters the building following the stairs to the first floor.'

'' He asked the first police officer''

Good day, my name is Detective John Coleman. Can you tell me where the office of Mr Carl Watkins please.'?

'Officer smiled and said:' we are waiting for you! I know who you are!'

Yes, follow this corridor down the end on the right is the office of Mr Carl!'

'John laughed then said:' Thank you, officer, very kind of you,!'

'John has walked down the corridor. He knocks on the door,'

'Yes who is!' Carl asked;'

John has opened the door:' Hi Carl It's me! I must say this place looking different as I remember!' said John:'

Carl has been sitting on his chair messing around with his working paper.'

Carl said:' Please John have a seat!' Yea there was some work in the building just a few years ago but everything else looks the same:' So did you have a rest?' Asked Carl;'

'John smiled: Oh yes! Everything is perfect. Hotel is nice and the room is ok! Thanks!'

John asked:' So where do you want me to start first?'

'Michael enters the room without knocking on the door;' He was holding some papers in his hand!' His eyes rolled around when he saw John sitting there:' He said:'

Oh, you must be the famous detective John!' His voice appeared to be very stressy!'

'Im Detective Michael." Nice to have you here with us!'

'He was trying to cover his stress by holding tight his paperwork in his hands:'

'John's eyebrows went tight, he was observing Michael.'

John said:' Hello Michael, nice to meet you too,!' What I would suggest is get on with work!'

'We have things to do!' he said sharply:'

John asked:' So Michael what have you found so far?'

'Carl was sitting there holding his cup of coffee in his hands.'

'Carl has interrupted John for a second then said;'

Michael has found that Anne who was killed didn't have any family members alive. The money she has earned the most of that money she gives to Daniel. Michael has also found where our Daniel works. So I would suggest that we better drive to San Jose to find this person.!'

' John was listening carefully to every word.'

John said sharply;' Let's go, guys! There is no time wasting!'

'Michael added:' I agree with sir, absolutely!'

'I forgot to say that the analysis from the forensic lab showed nothing.' we got the results yesterday.' whoever killed Anne Willson he covered his tracks very well !'

'John and Carl murmured at the same time.' Hmm....

John added: ' Unfortunately It's always like this! 'Well we will now proceed to the next stage of our case!'

'They left the office early that day. They have been driving to San Jose.!'

'During the drive, John has already created in his mind why the girl was killed. He already knew but he needed strong proof.'

'It has been a long drive to San Jose, a couple of hours at least. They have stopped a few times on the way to the Coastal area of San Jose.'

'Arriving at the coastal town of San Jose later in the afternoon Carl has to turn into the little road to find the parking space. He managed to park the car just in front of the building where the new movie was filming. They were looking for Daniel Harper."

'Getting closer to the building John has taken his dark sunglasses off.'

"In front of the building were standing security guys;' Tall guy was wearing a black suit. He was holding his hand tight very close to his chest.!'

'John has come first!' He pulls out from his left pocket the badge showing the security guy who is!'

'The tall guy looked at him sharply;' his face was flashing!'

'Carl and Michael just stepped behind.!'

Oh, so you are from the police department!' Guy has asked:'

John remains very comical:' he said:' yes we are!' we are looking for the actor Daniel Harper!'

'Let us in!' John has an order!'

'The guy didn't have many options so he let the Police in!'

'Carl and Michael were looking around! Were too many people working on the same film!'

'Many different departments on the set!'

'Little bald man was coming towards them!'

He has stopped in front of John Coleman asking!'

'Hi my name is Andrew and I'm the producer!' May I help you, Detective!' I have just been informed by the security that I have got Police visitors around!'

So how can I help you?' Andrew asked:'

'John has stretched his hair.' He said:

We are looking for Mr Daniel Harper! Can you call him please!"

Carl added: Mr Andrew we don't have time to play games around here. It is very important!'

'Andrew was looking pale!' he said:' Yes of course! Please follow me!'

'They were following Andrew around the filming set! There were too many people around, very noisy and hot!'

'Andrew pointed at the man who was sitting on the chair with dark hair.'

He said: That's Daniel over there!'

John added:' Thank you. We are not going to belong. We do need to ask a couple of questions to this guy!'

'Getting closer to Daniel, John has puffed his cigar.'

'Good day Mr Daniel!' A deep voice appeared behind Daniel's back!'

'Daniel turned around and in front of him he could see the tall man looking at him very sharply!'

Daniel said:' Yes It's me, I'm Daniel! And who are you?' he asked:'

John has shown him his Detective badge!'

'Daniel has looked somehow very upset having police in front of him.'

Daniel said:' Police, what a nice surprise?' he said:

John said in a casual tone:' Mr Daniel ! hmm do you know that your girlfriend Anne Wilson is dead!"

'Carl and Michael were standing there living with John to interrogate him.'

Daniel was shaking!' He was so upset that he couldn't say a word!'

'He has pulled his hair very strongly saying:'

What? When? Oh my god, she can be dead!!! 'He was screaming!' there were people around looking at him!' what the hell is going on!!!?'

'John didn't trust him. He knew him as an actor! He had a feeling that Daniel is involved in all of this!'

John said: Hm, Your girlfriend Anne has pushed two days ago from her balcony around 4 pm in the morning. When was the last time Anne?' 'John's eyes were looking sharply at him.'

'Daniel took a tissue to wipe his face covered in sweat.'

He answers;' I' saw her two nights ago. We had a wonderful time together. I left her a note on the kitchen table. We were supposed to met In the restaurant Lazy beer, but I have to go back to work so I left her a message before I left!' I have tried to call her but I couldn't reach her on the phone!'

Oh My God!!' I'm in shock!!'

John has litten his cigar!'

He asked:' Did you know that Anne left you a pile of money?'

'Daniel answered;' Yes I did! Oh, hold on! you think that I'm the one who killed my girlfriend for money!!! 'He was furious!' Is that what you think, Detective?' he asked;'

'There was a minute of silence.'

John said;' Look, Mr Daniel! We have a murder here. You were involved in a romantic relationship with Anne! Your girlfriend didn't have a family; her parents died in a car accident!' And on top of this she left you a pile of money!!!' 'John has been more and pushier!'

'Daniel appears to be more stressful!'

'He screamed! I didn't kill Anne!!!!' I loved Anne!'

'Detective wait. I think what you are saying about the Anne family that's not true!

'Anne had a sister! She disappeared a long time ago somewhere! As far as I know, she never contacted Anne. I think her name was Margaret!'

Anne never wanted to talk much about her!' That's all I know, detective!'

'Carl and Michael were looking at each other!'

'John was scratching his eyebrow thinking thoughtfully.'

John said:' This is something to investigate! Anyway, we will need you Mr Daniel, so I suggest not leaving the town till all of this is not over. Thank you for your collaboration with us. We will be in touch. Have a nice day!

'They left the place.'

'This is getting better and better: said John!'

'Carl asked:' what do you think John is, is he lying or telling the truth! Who the hell is Margaret!'?

'John thought to himself:'

John said: If he is telling the truth, it could be Margaret that she murder his own sister!'

We have to find Margaret!!'

'Carl was pulling the car keys from his pocket.'

John said thoughtfully:' I think Daniel is hiding something! It would be good if we put 2 police officers to follow him!' What do you think Carl? John has asked:'

Carl said:' Ok no problem John! But what do you think he is hiding from us!?' Carl asked:'

'John has puffed smoke in the air:' he said: First of all he didn't show up that day when he was supposed to meet with Anne. The night when Anne was murdered. He disappears. He did say he was going to call her and he probably did! He creates a perfect alibi for himself!! The second thing he said was that Anne had a sister Margaret who disappeared somewhere. And so far we know that Anne did not have sisters or brothers! Why would he say something like this! He wants us to go down the wrong path to look for a non-existing person. The third thing is Anne has left him a pile of money which makes him look like someone who wanted to get rid off so all the money would be on his name! But of course, we will check if Anne really had a sister!' That's the next thing we have to do and of course, we have to put 2 police officers to follow Daniel.'

'Michael added:' I think sir you are right!'

'Carl was looking a bit confused.' He said:' hmm ok John.let's do it!!'

'Driving back to San Francisco detective Carl has received a phone call. He has stopped on the first corner to answer the phone,'

'He answered;' Hello! Hey Mike It's me! What's up?

'It was another police officer on the phone.'

'Just find another dead body under the bridge!' Where are you Carl?!' Mike asked:'

Carl responds rapidly: Thanks for calling me! We will be there in 2 hours!;

'Carl has put the phone down, he was looking at John!'

John and Carl were listening with interest:'

'John asked:' what is going on Carl?'

Carl said slowly:' Oh man! We got another murder down the bridge!'

'John murmured;' I think this all connects!'

'Carl asked' do you honestly think that this second murder is connected to the first one?'

John said: When the man's neck is in danger, he doesn't stop to think !'

Michael smiled; he asked: What does it mean? Some kind of enigma?'

Carl said:' Soon we will find out!'

'Arriving at the crime scene John could see that the man had been shot two times in the back.'

By the way, how he was looking appeared to be a very tall man in the late '40s.

John has been looking around in case he could find something around the area.'

The body stood there probably for one day or more. The next thing was to find out who was that man who had been killed.

'Close to the water John has noticed a small green lighter standing there as someone has lost it, he picks it up very slowly and he puts the object into the plastic bag as a piece of evidence. He didn't tell Carl or Michael.'

He had a feeling what was going on.'

The forensic there was there!

'Carl felt so tired his heart problem was giving him so much trouble'

'Carl asked:' Hey John, would you like to go somewhere for a drink?' I'm pretty tired of this shit!'

John has answered straightaway:' Yes of course!' are you ok?' he asked;

'Carl's face was flashing in red:' he responds:' I feel so tired. It's been a long day! Apart from that, I would like to resolve this case. I know you have your family waiting for you at home man!

I'm sorry to put you in all this mess!'

'His voice sounds tired.'

John answered;' Hey I'm happy to work with you again Carl! I think we will soon resolve this case! Don't worry about my wife, she is perfectly fine. She knows my job is too hectic!

Come on, let's go for a drink! I think you need one more than I do!'

'John Coleman was smiling.'

'It was a conversation between two good old friends.'

John Coleman and Carl were working together for years in the same department in San Francisco.'

When John met his wife they moved together in New York then John was transferred to the new job!'

But two old friends have never lost their connection.'

'Carl has stopped the car in front of the Zam Zam bar in 1633 High St.'

'They sit close to the window.' There were many people around, apparently a very busy place.'

'Carl ordered a glass of brandy and John had a whisky.'

John has been looking for a packet of cigarettes! as he couldn't find any he walked to the bar to buy one.'

'He offered to Carl one:'

John has asked:' So Carl what do you think about this Daniel? I mean Anne's boyfriend!?'

'Carl responded:' Hmm, I would say he is hiding something! There is too much coincidence involved! Her death, then the money, then this guy who we just found under the bridge!' the sudden disappearance of Daniel. What I mean is he didn't show up for dinner with Anne. That was the same night when Anne was murdered.' The mysterious appearance of Margaret Anne's sister!'

'The two-man eyed each other.'

John said; Hmm, I think the same Carl as you!' I do have some pretty good ideas!'

'Carl's eyebrows went up:'he asked:' What have you got in mind John?'

John answered;' Shall I say I will live it as a surprise!' We have to find Anne's sister 'Margaret' and we do need to send 2 cops to follow Daniel!' I would like to do it now if you don't mind!?'

'Yes of course;' said Carl.

As a matter of fact, the medication man said that Anne had been murdered around 3 pm to 4 pm in the morning!' Our forensic team couldn't find anything. I'm wondering if we are going to have some luck tomorrow about the 2 murder occurred down the bridge.' Carl said in a low voice;'

'The ashtray on the table was slightly filled with smoked cigars.' The waiter came to collect empty glasses:' More drinks guys?!' waiter asked:'

'John raised his eyebrow' he asked:' Carl do you want one more drink?'

Carl said:' Yes, why not!

'Carl looked at the waiter' he said:' Yes please, one more brandy for me and one glass of whisky!' thank you!'

'As it was late afternoon, the bar started to fill with people.' Carl was feeling tired so he offered to John to drive him back to the Hotel.'

'Tomorrow we have a busy day ahead' said John!'

Carl responds;' yes we do! Lets' go now. I will give you a drive back to the Hotel!'

'They left the Bar moving slowly to the car.' Carl felt a bit drunk but somehow he managed to drive back.'

'During the drive, John said:' You know Carl, I'm a well known professional man, and I do take my job very seriously.

'We will resolve these two murders! Tomorrow we will find out who the dead man is on the bridge!'

'I agree, absolutely with you John!' said Carl.'

'Carl has stopped the car in front of the Hotel.'

'He said;' John, I will see you tomorrow morning at the office! thanks for everything!'

John Coleman responded:' Sure man I will be there on time!' Have a rest Carl you need one!!'

'John has turned and walks back to the Hotel puffing his cigar very slowly.'

'Next morning 3 detectives met each other at 8 am in the office.'

'Carl has put 2 more cops on duty to follow the Daniel'

'They finally had results about the 2 murder down the bridge.'

'The evidence has shown that the man who has been shot twice in the back was a drug dealer; he has had a very dark past. He would do anything for money!'

'His name was Craig Watson.'

'The little green lighter that John Coleman has found very close to the dead body has been sent away to his good friend in the San Francisco forensic department together with the note that Daniel has left on the kitchen table the night Anne was murdered.' John has kept that as a secret from Carl and Michael.' He knew very well what he was doing!'

'He suspects how things have gone but he needs strong proof.'

'Carl said:' I sent 2 more cops to follow Daniel! What we know so far is that he is working all the time on the film set!' Nothing unusual!'

John scratched his eyebrow:' Hm wait for Carl! The news will come to us very soon, believe me, I know what I'm talking about!'

Michael added:' What you two are talking about!'? We got 2 murders to resolve. This is not a guessing game sir John!' 'he appeared to be very irritated!'

'John looked at him;' he asked;' Michael are you always so stressed? If you are! then this job isn't for you!'

'Carl smiled.' He was holding a cup of coffee in his hands:' he said: Oh yes! Michael has a problem with controlling his anger! He is not patient!' He is always like this but he is doing a good job I must say!' he is still young!'

John added:' Let me tell you young man being the detective you need to learn how to control your own emotions. When I started my career as a detective during my working experience I learned to deal with different people and different murders. What we are doing It's not an easy job. It is not a guessing game It is more like resolving a puzzle. You need to have eyes to not miss any important details, you have to look people in the eyes observing their body movement because this is very important and the best thing is to keep comm.!'

Carl said:' Very true John!' I agree with you!'

'Michael was standing there listening very carefully.' he was starting to realize the point of the message.'

'There was not much to do in the office that day except wait.'

Carl puffed his cigar;' he said: Strange this Craig who we found dead under the bridge he didn't have any family I'm just looking at his profile!' What a scam bag!'

'I wish that all these trashy people were locked behind the bars!'

It's disgusting what they are doing!'

John said:' Hmm yes man! Who can catch them all Carl! There are too many!'

'There are people migrating from all over the world looking for a better life but what they do to make money is horrible.'

Michael added:' I'm going back down to my office, Carl! If you need me to call me!'

See you John!' 'He shut the door and walked away.'

Carl and John were standing there, eyeing each other!'

Carl asked:' So should we take a break? Early lunch?' Here is not much to do!'

John said: I have got a better idea. We should go check the Apartment of Mr Craig!'

'Maybe we can find something important inside the apartment!'

'Carl murmured to himself!' Hm ok then! Let's go!'

'Carl has put his jacket on and he was checking his pockets looking for the car keys.'

'On the office desk were too many papers hanging around.'

'He looked around, he didn't like any mess!'

He murmured to himself:' Oh I have to clean this messy table!'

'He and John went across the corridor down the stairs.'

'The road traffic was so busy. It took them one hour to reach 6 Avenue.

The car turned left then stopped in front of the big building!

Mr Craig was on the 5th floor.' First came John!'

They took the stairs to the 5 floors! As they did not have keys, of course, John had a special little tool to open the door of the apartment.'

'It was a very old building, not very nice from inside! Very dark!' Carl thought;'

'Was that kind of area where most of the black people were living.'

'Not a very secure place to hang around.'

'Loat's of drugs and prostitute were outside during the night time'

'Inside of the apartment was so messy, dirty and the smell was covering the whole place!'

'John has started to look around the bedroom.'

'Carl said in a low voice:' Hey John I'm going to check the kitchen to see what I can find!'

What a horrible dark place!; John added:'

'They were checking each drawer hoping to find anything that would help them to resolve this case sooner.'

'Unfortunately nothing has been found there!

'The only thing John found was a plastic bag filled with white powder!'

John put his finger into the plastic bag to taste what kind of drug it was!'

' cocaine was hanging inside a bag he thought to himself worth a lot of money.'

'He passes the plastic bag to his friend Carl.'

How awful:' said Carl!'

John scratched his hair:' he said: let's go man!'

'Carl has agreed with John.' There was nothing there, just a horrible smell.'

'Carl said; I got to call Michael on the way back, see what he is doing!

'He drew a deep breath!'

John added: let's buy some food! I'm " damn hungry now!'

'Carl responded:' Oh sure I'm starving.'

'During the drive, Carl has received a phone call.'

There were 2 cops put out on duty to follow Daniel.'

'Carl has answered the phone.'

Hi, guys said Carl;' What do you have? Any news?'

Peter responded: Hey Carl. We are going around and around following Daniel all day.

He was ok for a while, but we can see how he just went out with a very attractive blonde woman from his apartment.

We can't see her from up close but she is very pretty!'

'Carl puffed his cigar:' he said:' Thanks very much! Keep doing your job. Find as much you can about the blonde women!' he ordered!

'John Has been listening to his bear.'

'Carl asked again' Is there anything else I shoulda known!'

'There was a pause '

Peter responded:' No detective Carl that would be all for now. Anyway, we will keep following Daniel and keep you informed whatever we find out about this guy!'

'Carl has put his phone down and stared at John.'

So what did they find out?'! Asked John:'

'John has been very curious, he wanted to know but deep down he knew who the blonde women were hanging out with Daniel.'

'Carl's eyebrows went up:' He responded: well they saw Daniel coming from his apartment with an attractive blonde woman. I told them to keep working on it!

Maybe is just another actress! It would be too weird to see Daniel with other women knowing how poor Anne has lost her life!' said Carl:'

John smiled:' He said: Eh Carl! I think It's more than that.'

Those two murders are very well planned and I will prove that very soon!' John said very sharply'

Carl asked:' What do you mean by that John? Is there something you have forgotten to tell me?'

John said in a casual tone;' You will find out soon!'

Carl's eyes were smiling: Ah , knowing you I'm sure this case will be resolved very soon!'

Anyway, I'm really happy to have you here John.' whatever you're not telling me I will leave it as a surprise!'

'Carl has always known how John has kept his little tricks till the end.

He left most of the job to him to resolve.'

John was brilliant.' Carl thought:'

John Coleman added:' hey what about our food!?' I'm starving!'

'Tonight I will have to call my wife.' said John!'

Carl responded:' I know the place where we can stop to have some food!

The restaurant is just great! It's Italian food! I love it! They served Seafood if you fancy? Carl asked:'

John responded in a casual way:' Thanks, man! That would be great. We had a long working day! Lets'go!'

Carl added:' It's not very far from here! It's on 30th St.'

'Carl has turned left driving very fast!'

'It was coming at 6 pm in the evening. They were stuck in horrendous traffic!'

'The phone has been ringing and ringing for 3 times during the drive.'

'Carl has been concentrating on the road and the traffic in front of him he couldn't pick up the bloody phone!' His eyes pointed to John saying!'

'John, please can you answer the phone!'

' John has picked up the phone.' he answered:' Hello Detective John Coleman is here.!?

Michael said:' Oh hi John! Where is my boss? He asked;'

John puffed his cigar;' he said:' Hi Michael! Carl is driving at the moment he can't answer the phone. Any urgency? John Coleman has asked:'

Michael responded:' No, no urgency. Can you tell Carl I'm finished for today? I 'm going home. Any news regarding a case? Michael asked:'

John said:' Yes we do have some news about Daniel. Don't worry Michael, you go home now! Everything is ok!' John smiled:'

'Michael felt some kind of relief.' he said: Thanks, John! Bye for now! I will see you both tomorrow morning at the office.'

John responds;' Yes, see you at the office.'

'John has put the phone down ending the conversation.'

'Carl asked:' What he wanted?'

John responded:' He just wanted to say how he had finished his job for today! that's all!' He asked if we had any news. Anyway, you did hear what I was saying to him.'

Carl murmured to himself:' Oh yes! Michael does this all the time. He has to call every time he is done with his job!' Always the same with Michael!' 'Carl smiled!'

John added:' I think Michael is a very intelligent young man! He takes his job very seriously.'

Carl said:' Hmm Yes. Michael is very good at his job! But he has to learn how to control his own emotions and anger.!' Sometimes It's really hard to work with him.'

'Carl was looking around for the parking space.'

'Two detectives came inside into the Ciccia restaurant which was full of people.' It is a very famous restaurant in San Francisco.'

They ordered two big fish on the grill with baked potatoes and a pile of fresh salad going very well with the red bottle of Vintage Bordeaux wine!'

'John and Carl ended up very smashed that night. Just like in the old times! They didn't talk much about the job, most of the conversation went on about their private lives.'

'Two old friends were hanging out together after a very long time.'

'Next day the wind picked up. You could smell the rain in the ear.'

'Carl gets up from the bed and picks up the glass of water together with medication.

'He swallows the tablet in one go.'

'He didn't feel like going to work this morning.' feeling lazy:' he murmured to himself.'

'It was already coming at 8 am.'

'He knew there was a lot to do in the office.'

'He collects his car keys and shuts the door. He was in a rush,'

'He thought to himself: last night was great but too much for me I guess! Hmm, I'm getting older!'

He smiled to himself:'

'On the way to work, he has stopped to buy fresh sandwiches and a cup of coffee!'

He murmured to himself:' I'm going to be late!'

'Rolling slowly in the traffic road he put the radio on. It was something to entertain him!

'He was getting closer to the police station. Luckily his job was not so far from the place where he lived.'

'He has parked the car in the same place as usual.'

'Running to the stairs he has stopped to say hello to Michael who has already been there working.'

'He noticed John Coleman wasn't there.'

'He opened the door from his office, he sat on his chair, poured the cup of coffee and ate the first sandwich.'

' He was thinking to give a call to John Coleman when the phone rang twice;'

'Carl picked the phone and answer;'

'John Coleman was on the line;'

John said in a casual tone:' Hi Carl! I'm not going to be able to come today to the office.

Something Important has happened. I will call you as soon as I get some news!'

'Carl drinks his coffee he asked:' What news John? Where are you?'

John murmured: you will know very soon!' Give some time!'

'John hasn't been very specific in his words.' Carl thought:'

Carl said:' You are doing some investigation aren't you?

John responded thoughtfully:' Yes Carl! I will see you soon!'

'Them conversation has ended. Carl knew that John was about to discover the killer.'

'He had a feeling.'

'He put his cigar in the ashtray and walks downstairs to the Michael office.'

'In the meantime, John has got the results from the forensic department in San Francisco;'

'As he was suspecting everything was matching.'

'He put together all the puzzles. He knew!'

John walked down the street on 20 st avenue he picked the phone up and called Carl!'

As he couldn't reach Carl's office he phoned Michael!'

His eyebrows went up and down! What the hell!' where are they?' hm!'

'Finally, Michael had answered the phone!'

John said:' Hi Michael. I was trying to call Carl's office. Where is he? He asked:

Michael responded:' Hey John, not to worry Carl is here in my office! Did you get something? He asked:'

John puffed his cigar in the air:' Yes! We are going to San Jose now! He said sharply:'

He added: there is no time to waste. Tell Carl to inform the police we do need more police officers!' Hurry up, Michael!' John has given an order:'

'John said: I'm at 20 st avenue waiting here! Hurry up!'

'Michael has put his phone down.'

'Two men eyed each other'

Carl knew that John was very close to resolving this case.'

The two detectives left in a hurry at the Police station .'

Carl has informed the rest of the police team.'

'Arriving at 20 st avenue John has been waiting there smoking his cigar.'

"Closing the door behind him: Carl asked:' what is going on John?'
'Michael was staring at him.' He didn't know what was going on!'
John said in a low voice;' I know who murdered Anne Willson.'
'It was all part of the plan Carl!'
Wait and see!'
Carl has scratched his heir saying:' Hm I knew you will resolve this case!' but I would like to know how you did it this time! I'm curious!'
'Anyway I send more police cars over there as you asked:' Carl added:'
'Michael was driving the car to San Jose; he didn't say a word.'
'He thought how Detective John Coleman came to the solution so quickly.'
John said:' Thanks, man! I believe that our Daniel must be working on the set.
It is the perfect place to arrest him!'
Carl asked: Are you sure that Daniel is a killer?'
John murmured;' Oh yes I'm. The whole way he planned everything it was really hard to put the puzzle together.' Believe me, Carl!'
John carries on talking:' The motive of this murder is money. Apart from that, there is love involved as well.'
'Carl was stretching his legs.' he asked: what love? With who?
'Michael was listening very carefully, he had to concentrate on the road.'
John's eyes were smiling;' he responded in a deep voice;' Oh Carl wait and see till we get there.'
Carl said: Yea man as always you are full of surprises!' Nobody can get away working with you. I Know that very well.' That's why you are a brilliant detective.'
'John has smiling'
'After two hours of a long drive, they finally were getting closer to San Jose.'

'Michael was looking where to park the car.'

Detective John and Carl came out from the car waiting for Michael.'

'There was ready to enter inside the building'

'The same security guy was standing there smoking a cigar.'

'He recognises them, at first sight, he couldn't pretend.

Oh, good day detectives;' the tall guy has said:

'He opens the door to let them in.'

'They have been looking for Daniel Harper around.'

'Carl has just seen him sitting there talking to the producer.'

'He taps John on the shoulder saying:' Hey John look, Daniel is over there. Let's go!'

'John came first.'

He said: Hi Mr Daniel. Can we talk somewhere in private?

'Pointing with his finger at the state caravan below:'

'Daniel's face turned into a pale yellow color.'

'His voice starts to shake very slowly.'

He asked:' What a surprise, detectives. I didn't expect you here anymore!

'Yes we can talk in my private caravan over there. I hope It's not gonna take long! I have to get back to my work as a detective.' first

John said sharply;' Oh not at all. But I do have two questions for you, Mr Daniel.'

'Daniel was looking very upset; he was trying to cover his stress.'

He asked:' Detectives, can I offer you a drink? He poured a big glass of brandy in his own glass.'

John answered;' No thank you.'

'Michael and Carl were there listening.'

John scratched his bear:' he asked:' So Mr Daniel the first question is. Where are you hiding Miss Margaret? And my second question is how did you think to get away with this?

Michael and Carl eyed each other without saying a word.' everything

'Daniel's face turned from pale into a hot red.' Holding his brandy in his left hand the glass was starting to shake slightly.'

John noticed at first.'

Daniel responded;' what? What Margaret!' I don't know any Margaret! He shouted:'

John said in a low voice:' Mr Daniel Harper, your arrogance has insulted me. But not only me in this room. You see you're insulting my colleagues as well.'

Let me be more specific, I will tell you how you plan everything.

'Daniel shouted hysterically:' I don't know what you are talking about!'

'The police cars were getting closer.'

'John's eyebrows went up as he put his cigar in the ashtray.'

John pulled from his left pocket a green lighter holding in the plastic bag and pointing to Daniel's face.'

'He carries on talking;' So do you see this item? Let me start from the beginning.'

On the night when your girlfriend Anne was murdered, that night you left a note on her kitchen table saying that you are not going to be able to meet with her.

So what did you do next, you went to meet with Mr Craig the drug dealer and Miss Margaret the sister of Anne had paid this guy a pile of money to murder the Anne.

After that, you came back into your apartment as nothing had happened.!

'Daniel was so upset, he couldn't control his emotions any more!

'Daniel said; Oh yes and how will you prove this detective? Asked Daniel:

John smiled:' he said: well pretty easy I would say. You see this green lighter, this lighter is yours, Mr Daniel. Shall I say! As Mr Craig didn't feel happy about the amount of money you paid him and he wanted more, you arranged to meet him down the bridge. You were fighting with him, then shot him twice in his back and of course, during the fight, you lost this little green lighter on the floor. So when I sent the analysis, this lighter was perfectly matching the note that you left on the kitchen desk when Miss Anne was murdered.'

Oh my, said Daniel:' Bravo, bravo detective. He was applauding with his hands!

John has put his hat down the table;' he asked: So where is Miss Margaret? You and Miss Margaret knew each other for a very long time. That's how you meet her sister Anne. Even as Miss Margaret disappeared for a very long time she always followed her younger sister Anne. She knew everything." so the two of you had planned everything in advance. It was all about the money and I guess love triangle.!'

'Carl and Michael were surprised:'

'Daniel was standing there in shock. His face was sweating like a hell."

Someone has just opened the door.'

'The attractive blond women appeared in front of them.

'Her blue eyes were cold like she didn't have any emotions at all.'

'She was smoking the cigar.'

Detective John Coleman said:' I guess you are Miss Margaret!'

'Margaret was smiling cynically;' she responded:' Yes I'm Margaret. Are we done here?'

'Police were standing there. They came just on time.'

Detective John Coleman pointed with his finger saying to the police officers: 'Take them both.'

'Carl and Michael were very pleased:'

Carl asked:

When did you find the green lighter?'

John smiled;' ah well that's the little secret I kept away from you!'

Carl responded in a casual way:' I knew you were hiding something, haha

'After a couple of days, Carl was driving Detective John Coleman to the airport.'

'Two friends were standing there waiting for the flight to New York.'

Carl said: Well John thank you for everything. Who would think that the sister of Anne was involved in all of this? I guess Daniel was deeply in love with that cold bitch.'

Carl murmured: Poor Anne!'

'John responded by puffing his cigar.' You know the murder always has a strong motive unless a serial killer is involved where we are dealing with a Psycho but that is different.'

Carl said: very true John!' Well, I hope to see you soon! You and I should ketchup sometimes just as friends without involving the job!'

John smiled, saying:' I agree with Carl, just like in old times.'

'Two detectives said goodbyes.'

An FBI agent John Coleman has been invited by the police from France-Paris to help in the investigation of serial murders. All victims that police have found have been murdered in very similar ways. The killer was strangling victims then bathed and dressed their bodies.

Inspector Larsen said:"This case Isn't easy at all , we do need help! I have got a bad feeling about these murders.

John Coleman is a professional FBI agent with many years of experience in catching serial killers. It was a pleasure for him to be invited by inspector Larsen to help in resolving this complex case.

John asked:' Hey, Larsen, it is so nice to see you after such a long time!' How are you?

Larsen said:' Welcome back, John! We do have some more people working on this case , but I do need you here as well. I' don't like what I see in these murders, there is something different.'

John asked:' yes I do understand you . Please, show me where the last victim remains? So I can start to work on the killer profile!'

Larsen said:' of course, follow me please!' Until now we have found three bodies killed in the same way.' The killer strangled the victims, then bathed them and dressed them and left them on the side of the road.' I do not know what to think!

John said:' oh , I will try to do my best so we can catch this guy. This is my job!

'John has examined the body of the first victim and he founds out that the victim was raped before she was killed and dumped on the side of the road. All three victims are young women between 20-25 years old.'

John said:' I must say that each victim had the round circle on the left leg, it was almost perfectly cut with a knife.' what I do want to say is that it will be more of this.'

Larsen said:' oh shit, I never seen something like this in my career, that's why I called you to come and help us with the investigation.'

John said:' In my opinion, we should start to investigate what does it mean those circles found on the victims bodies that is the first track that is leading us to the killer mind.'

Larsen said:' I agree with you . It would be good to do some research to see what we can find.'

John said:' Yes, I will meet you tomorrow in the office.'

Larsen replied:' thanks John, see you tomorrow!'

'John has spent many hours looking at the pictures of dead bodies trying to understand every single detail, or perhaps he was missing something important.'

'Following day he meets with Larsen in the office and the rest of the team of detectives.'

John added:' these murders are planned ,our killer is choosing the victims by observing them for a while before he decides to kill them. As we can see in the pictures he chooses young women and all of these women have something in common.' He makes perfect cut circles on the left legs. What I'm trying to say is that we have to find out what these circles are and that is a first step to do in this investigation.

'I wouldn't be surprised if we discover another victim soon!'

Larsen said:' well guys we better get on with our job. We are dealing here with the real psychopath. 'Back o work , back to work!'

Larsen added:" It's really good to have you hear John.' this is a very hard case , as I said before we do need more people.'

John replied:' yes we do need more people. I will go today to check some details regarding these circles

and see what I can find .'

Larsen said:' ok , thank you!'

'John has been spending the time in the library. What he did find out there were nine circles of hell in the book 'Dante's inferno' which are limbo, greed, violence, lust, anger , fraud , gluttony , heresy and treachery. He was now convinced there are going to be six more murders. He was just about to call Larsen when his phone rang.'

John answered and said:' hello Larsen, any news? I just found out something very interesting!'

Larsen added:' hi John we have just found another victim can you please hurry up!'

John said: I'm coming. " He was driving very fast."

'Arriving at the crime scene he could see there was another woman about the same age as the previous victim.'

John asked:' can we talk in private?'

Larsen replied:' of course. I can't believe what I see. I'm waiting for the results to come out about the first three victims we found. It should be done today. Oh god it is the same memo, same everything.' The killer is choosing very carefully which women he will kill.

John said:' I'm afraid there are going to be five more murders.' Larsen looked at him and asked:' what do you mean by that ?

John replied:" Today in the library I found out there are nine circles of hell in the 'Dante's inferno' book , so I'm sure the killer will kill five more women.'

Larsen said: ' oh , how can we stop him.' we don't have any single details about the killer , we don't have anything at all. I have never seen anything like that in my life!' 'Larsen seems very upset.'

John said:' when we do have those results today from the lab we will know more about the victims .

I'm sure these women have something in common.'

Larsen replied:' I' don't know what to think.'

John said:' Maybe someone can help us from the prison? What do you think?

Larsen replied:' yes but who?

John said:' what I would like to do is.' we must have a criminal who has been killed in the same way or similar way. These psychopaths usually have someone who admires them ,someone who has committed a similar crime, so they try to get in contact with them.'

Larsen replied:' I can check but I'm not sure it will work! We can try.' 'Couple of hours later the results came from the lab.'

'John, Larsen and detective Anne came into the lab.' Larsen asked:"So what do we have here?

' The first victim identified is Marie Anttoniete she was a school teacher ,the second victim is Elaine Monroe she was a solicitor , the third victim is Katrine Rene she was a doctor and the last victim is identified as a school teacher again.'

'I can say by observing these bodies and by the autopsy all these women are killed in the same way.' And they all have something in common, they all have had a very successful career.'

John said:' this is very interesting. My question is why the killer is choosing women with a successful career? It is very confusing. We know he will kill five more times I'm sure of it. What we have more in this case is nothing ! No witness, no fingerprints , nothing!'

Larsen added:' I agree with you we don't have nothing. He is very clever . He kills one woman every week one women so we can expect every week to find one more victim.'

Mr Larsen told detective Anne:' we have just received a phone call from the women . She is convinced that she saw the killer.

Larsen said:' Oh finally something in this fucking case! Larsen asked:' What is the name of the witness?

Anne replied:' Her name is Mrs Claire Durset.' John added:' finally let's go!'

'The police cars were driving fast.'

Larsen said:' hopefully this time we will catch this guy.'

'Arriving at the place of the witness, detective John and Larsen went together inside the house.' Larsen said:' Good day Mrs Claire my name is detective Larsen and this is my associate Mr John. 'we have some questions to ask you.'

Larsen asked: Mrs Claire, what can you tell us about the killer, what makes you think that this is a killer we are looking for?'

Mrs Claire replied:' I have been watching all of this on the news. The last victim was my dear neighbor Clarisee Houston. She was a school teacher. She has recently met a man, he was his boyfriend , she told me. She didn't date him for a very long time after she was killed.'

Larsen asked:' So Mrs Claire you think that this person could be the killer?

Mrs Claire replied:' Inspector I'm not sure. What I can say is you can try to find him . It could be the man who killed Clarisse. I'm just trying to help.'

John asked:' Can you describe to us what he looks like?

Mrs Claire replied:' as I know , Clarisse told me he is a doctor and he works in the Hospital ' Bichat Claude -Bernard', his name is Philip Duncan.'

Larsen said:' thank you Mrs Claire this is what we are looking for. Many Thanks for your time and collaboration with us. You were very helpful.'

Mrs Claire said:' Please do not tell the doctor that I sent you!' Larsen replied:' oh no, don't worry.'

'Detectives they left the house of Mrs Claire'

Larsen and John were not sure that this guy is a killer. Something in this case wasn't very clear.' John said:' I'm not sure we are on the right path. The doctor can't be the killer!'

Larsen replied:' we will see what he is going to tell us.' I know how you feel, we are all getting tired of this case. Soon we will find the next victim.'

John replied:' probably in two days, I would say. And we are nowhere near him and he knows that.' Larsen added:' maybe I should bring some more people to work on this case ,don't get me wrong John

but we still don't have anything . We don't know what he looks like, where to find him and stop him ,I mean catch him. The only thing I know is that soon he will kill again and he is somewhere out there free.' John replied:' yes I know .I'm sorry I can't help you with this more but I'm doing what I can.' Larsen replied:' Of course you do John. I didn't mean that. You are my best friend and I do have full confidence in you and the work you do here.'

'Maybe if I have two FBI profilers this case could be solved sooner. Maybe we are missing something important.'

John said: ' let's go, we are here in hospital.'

'Good day nurse said John:' we are from the police. We are looking for the doctor Philip Duncan. Can you tell us where we can find him?'

'The nurse replied:' oh yes follow me please.

'Mr Duncan was sitting in his office.'

'She opened the door and said:' hello doctor, police are here they would like to speak with you.' 'Detectives enter the room.'

Larsen said:' hello Mr Duncan we do have to ask you some questions!' 'Mr Duncan was looking very curious.'

Doctor asked: yes of course please have a seat. How can I help you today, detective?

Larsen sat down and asked: have you been having a romantic relationship with Clarisse Houston? Is that correct?

Doctor said: oh yes we have been together . Clarisse is a very nice woman.

John asked:' where have you been last week between 7pm till 9pm?

Doctor said:' I've been having a Conference . Can I ask what happened? Why all of these questions?

John asked again:' can you prove you have been at the conference?

Doctor was very agitated , he asked:' what is all about I would like to know?!'

Of course I can prove to you where I was that night, as I already said I was at the conference.' Larsen said: Mr Duncan your girlfriend has been murdered last week. We are looking for the serial killer.'

'Doctor was shocked.'

He added:' oh my dear god . I didn't know anything. Who would kill Clarisse?

'He was very upset.'

Larsen said: we are working hard to catch the killer . I would like to say if you remember anything during your relationship with Clarisse please do call us. Until then have a nice day , goodbye!'

John said:' I did told you the doctor is not our killer. He is too clever to be caught by us. He is messing around with us.'

'During the drive they received another call, and a new victim has been found.' 'That was the sixth victim found . She was dumped and left on the side of the road.' The case was getting more complicated,'

John said:' He will kill three more women. Something is very strange in these murders.'

All victims are killed in the same way , they are all women and they all have good working careers. Our killer is looking like a Casanova.'

Larsen asked:' Hold on, what did you just say? '

John said:' Yes, like a lover Casanova. Classic murders.

Larsen added:' yes you are right. We can checklist of the art galleries. The way how our killer is

Choosing the women and the way how he kills them is matching with the description of Casanova.

Well done John. Now we are getting closer.

John said:' I hope this will work!

Larsen said:' me too. We will print all list of the art galleries, check the names and if we are lucky it

will take us to our killer.'

John added:' I agree with you.'

'The killer is talking to himself.'

'Oh dear mother you did make a monster of me. I hope you can see all my art work. You would be very proud of me. I still remember how you abused me, how my stepfather raped me and you didn't believed me. Listen to me listen you bitch I hate you. After suffering years from your abuse I have grown up to hate each woman and each woman should be punished. Tonight I will kill again , oh mother these things are making me so happy. I'm the killer and all these women are mine victims. Police they will never catch me. I'm too clever for them.'

'Larsen, John and the rest of the team were looking into each gallery, checking the names of each artist in town.'

John added:'' I still haven't found anything. Hey Larsen have you found something?

Larsen replied:' no nothing . Oh wait, maybe I do have something.

Larsen shouted;' Anne please can you check the name Julian Burton. See what you can find on him and

bring me the report over here in my office!

Anne said: yes sir!

'After a while police from Spain phoned up to say they were having nine murders in Madrid.' 'That happened a year ago so everything is matching this murders in Paris. So our killer is the same person. He is traveling across Europe and killing women.

Larsen said; I want all my detectives here in my office, now!

John asked:' what happened?'

Larsen said: Soon you will find out . We are having a big problem here.

'All the detectives came into Larsen's office.'

Larsen asked:' are we all here?

I just received news from the Spanish police department that they are dealing with the same case as we are. This is the same killer we are trying to catch here in Paris.' We are having a serious problem. This guy has already killed more than 15 women.'

Larsen asked:' Anne, did you find out anything about Julian Burton?

Anne said:' I was just about to do it but you called us to come into your office sir.

Larsen said: Anne you go now and bring me the report on my desk!

Anne said: yes sir.

John added: this is much worse than I expected to be.

'how we are going to put an end to this case .

Larsen said:' I don't know John. Only I know if this guy is in Paris which we think he is we have to catch him. I did say I have had a strange feeling about these murders.'

John added: yes I know . Things are getting out of control, I'm also wondering why the police from Spain just informed us about all of this.

Larsen said: I guess they wanted to help us. The killer is very smart . He is still out there free and

probably he is looking for the next victim.'

John said: he is very smart!

Anne said: Sir, here is the report about Julian Burton.

Anne added: I think he can be the killer, look at this file!

Larsen said: Thank you Anne. Oh this is very interesting..

John asked:' what have you got about Julian?

Larsen said: He was abused in his childhood by his own mother and stepfather. He is originally from Paris .

Larsen asked: John can you please check his address? We are going there now!

John replied: yes of course!

'All patrols of the police cars were driving to Julian Burton place.'

They searched all the houses. Inside the Apartment they have found strange items that the killer was using to strangle his victims. The stairs were leading into the basement . Detectives find three more dead bodies.'

The whole place smelled so horribly.

Larsen screamed: Killer he will run away!!

We need to block all the train stations ,buses and airport's.

Back to work ,we have to hurry up or he will escape!

Detectives have been working hard for a couple of months on this case but the serial killer was somewhere still free.

John said: It must be the way to catch this psychopath. I don't think he left the country. He must be hiding somewhere . What do you think about Larsen? John asked: Larsen replied: maybe John. It's hard to guess .

John said: look at his picture he does look like any normal guy. Who would ever say.. Hmmm Larsen added; yes very true almost every killer has got some kind of problem from childhood. In many years of my experience it has been proved. I hope we will manage to catch him

. Soon or later he will make mistakes. Something does not match with the investigation.

'After a while the real Julian Burton has come back home to Paris. He was away for a very long time.' He saw his apartment was all messed up so he called the police to report it.'

Detective Anne stood there shocked after she had received the phone call from Julian .

She ran into the detective office and said: oh inspector you want to believe this.

Larsen asked; what happened ?

Anne replied; oh Julian, the killer was just on the phone.' Larsen asked; what? Where is he?

Anne said: he is at his home, he complained that his apartment was found in mess so he called the

police.

Larsen stood up ready to go.

Hey John let's go . Larsen said:

Julian is here in Paris at his house.

John added: this is unbelievable. Let's go to grab this bastard!

Police cars were driving fast to arrest this psycho.

'Larsen puts his gun up , John is covering him from behind.'

'Julian opens the door and he sees two police officers with guns pointing at his face.' He didn't even have time to say something , he was arrested and taken to the police station. Larsen said: Julian you are arrested. You have killed 18 women so far.

Julian said very calmly: what? You must be kidding me. I never kill anyone in my life. You have the wrong guy!!"

John said:' I don't think so. Why did you kill these women?

Julian added; listen to me. I did not kill anyone! I just came back last night from Madrid. What I did was find out that my apartment was all messed up. That's why I called the police to report the incident. Maybe you are looking for my twin brother Jules.

'John and Larsen were shocked' your twin brother? Larsen asked:

Julian said: yes my twin brother. I never met him. We were separated as kids from birth. Jules has lived with his mother and I have been given away by my own mother. Anyway I grew up with a nice family. You can check what I'm saying . You can call my mother in Madrid and my wife. I do have two little children waiting at home.

Larsen added: we will check now! Do you know that your twin brother is a killer? Did he ever try to get in contact with you?

Julian replied: No never ! I can't believe he is the killer!'

John said; well he is a killer! He has killed nine women in Madrid and here in Paris.

Larsen added: please give me your personal details. I'm going to check now are you telling the truth. Wait here.'

John asked: How come you two have been separated from the birth?

Julian replied: I heard from my mother that my real mother was a horrible woman and her husband was a horrid man. I consider myself very lucky to have been given away.

At last I had a very nice childhood. I feel sorry for my twin brother.

John added: that must be horrible!

Larsen entered the room and said: thank you Julian. You can go . We will need your help to catch your twin brother. It looks like he has been using your apartment for a while. What I would suggest to you , don't go into your apartment , go to the hotel.

Julian has been shocked; Oh my god . Do you think he will come after me or my family?' John said: well this can happen. You have to collaborate with us all the time. We will move your family somewhere safe until all of this is over.

Julian added; this is very shocking for me. You must understand me. I never had a chance to meet with my brother and I always wanted to. It is very sad for me to find out that my brother is a possible killer. Larsen said: yes we can understand how you feel . It's not your fault!

Larsen added: we will help you to move to the hotel. You can feel safe there. We will also inform the

Spanish police department to move your wife and children somewhere safe. In my free time, I try to relax.

We are here to help if you need anything call us.

'Julian couldn't believe it.'

The same night from the hotel " La Reserve" he called his mother and wife Katharine.

'Katharine was shocked and surprise and the same time"

Katharine said: oh my darling that is shocking news! Your twin brother is a possible killer that police are looking for?

Julian added: don't worry Katharine . The police are working to put you and children somewhere safe. They should be there in the morning. Please prepare everything that you need . My mother, she will come to see you .

Katharine said: Ok no problem. Please take care of yourself. I hope to see you very soon. Love you .

Julian replied: good night my love. I will call you tomorrow! Love you too.

Katharine said: Bye -bye love.

" Julian couldn't sleep all night. He was trying to understand why his own brother could be the killer. He always wanted to meet him in person. Deep down he was wondering what he looked like, does it look like me?"

" At the police station."

Larsen said: hopefully this case will be over. I can't believe if Julian didn't turn up to be twin

brother of our possible killer we probably wouldn't have nothing to resolve this case.

This is a relief .

John said: oh yes . I finally understand this story. Julian has been adopted and Jules grew up with mother and stepfather in the abusive family. As how he suffered as a child he turned to be violent and he started killing innocent women. In the end it does make sense. Julian was very lucky."

Larsen said: yes indeed very lucky!

John added: I hope that Jules will not go after Julian's family. What makes me worried in this case is . Jules has already murder nine women in Spain, then he returned here in Paris to kill again . I think he will go after Julian's family, I think he was looking for Julian all this time."

Larsen said: very possible John. Hey I don't want to talk any more about this investigation for today. I'm very tired. I'm very happy that you are here , I appreciate a lot'. without your help it would be even harder to resolve this case.

John added: oh thank you very much. Sometimes I do think about why I choose to do this job. Always long working hours, away from your family and friends. But at the end you just realize there are other jobs not for me.'

Larsen said: hey John, we just received a phone call from the Spanish police department. They finally moved Julian's family somewhere out of the town.'

So far it looks good . I think I will go to visit Julian, would you like to come with me? 'Larsen asked:'

John added: yes of course, let's go!'

'Arriving at the hotel 'La Reserve'. Julian was sitting in the bar.' He was looking very worried.

'Larsen said: hello Julian how are you? We have news for you.'

'Julian looked at him then asked: hi detective. What news?

John asked: can we join you ?

Julian replied; oh yes please. Any news from my twin brother? 'he asked.'

Larsen said: no, we don't have news about your brother. We are here to inform you that your wife has been moved to a safe place.'

There will be few police officers looking after your wife. Everything is good so far.

Julian added: Yes I know. I have been talking to my wife this morning. I can't stay here much longer because my family needs me.

John said: yes we know that, but we need you here!'

Julian added: listen if you think that my brother is a killer, your job is to catch him!' I don't know how I can help you more. My wife needs me, my children need me too. I have to go back to my job soon. This is not a game.'

Larsen added: we know that Mr Julian. We don't know where your twin brother is. He can be anywhere in this town looking for a new victim! If he is after you ,we have a better chance to catch him.

Julian said: yes but what if he tries to kill my wife or my children?

John added:' I assure you, your wife is safe and your children.'

Julian said: I hope so. Please excuse me, I have things to do..

Larsen said: of course. If you need anything please call us.

Julian said: Thank you detectives. Bye -bye.

'Police were convinced that Jules was hiding somewhere in Paris.'

'After months and months of investigation and hard work police have discovered two more bodies . They have found the bodies close to the river. The bodies were left by the side of the road.' 'The man who found the bodies called the police.'

'Larsen and John went to the crime scene.'

John said: oh no two more bodies.

Larsen asked: what is the name of the witness?

John replied: his name is James Brown.

Larsen asked: Mr James what can you tell us. Have you seen the killer, how he looks?

James replied: someone has stopped the car . He or she was pulling something from the car, I didn't have a chance to see the face. I observed everything from my car.' It was dark. I think he dumped the bodies and left. Then I called the police.

John asked: did you see what car he was driving?

James replied: yes I think it was black ford , I'm sure it was an old ford!

John asked: how long was the car parked here?

James said: I would say about 20 minutes. Everything has happened so fast.'

Larsen said: thank you . If you remember any important details please call us. Here is my phone number.

John said: oh no two more bodies. We should call Julian!'

Larsen said: 'better to wait until our forensic team comes.'

John replied: ok .

'Larsen was pissed of , he had enough of this case,'

'John has called Julian.'

John said; Hi Julian it is me detective. How are you? We have just discovered two more bodies. I wanted you to know for your own safety.' We do believe he is here in Paris.

Julian replied: oh my god. That is horrible!! Thank you for telling me. Oh I can't believe this is happening.

John replied: I'm sorry Julian. You have to be very careful. We are not sure how long it will take for your brother to come after you. Your brother is a very dangerous man.' Julian said: thank you detective. I spoke to my wife today and she is ok.

John said; oh I'm glad to hear that.! Take care, bye -bye.

Julian added: Bye -bye detective.

Larsen asked: hey John come tonight to my place for dinner? My wife would love to meet you.

'Do you have any plans for tonight?

John replied; No plans !

Larsen added: excellent, let's go.

"Driving together to the Larsen house they have been talking about the investigation.' Larsen said; hi love. How are you? My good friend John is here.

Marie said: good to see you at home dear. Oh hi John it is very nice to meet you please come on in.

John added: very nice to meet you .

Marie said: my husband says all good things about you.

Marie added; I cook some chicken and potatoes in the oven.

Marie asked: John would you like a glass of vine or you prefer beer?

John said: vine would be fine. Thank you.

;They sat at the table.'

Marie asked: how is the investigation going?

Larsen added: oh love, we don't want to talk about the job!'

Marie replied: ok , no problem dear.

John said: we are getting very close to finishing this case.

John added: thank you for inviting me for dinner.

Marie added: Today I received a phone call from my mother. She said she can take children for two weeks.

Larsen said: oh wonderful news.

John added; that is the best thing . It's always a good feeling when our parents can help us.

'They laughed together'

Marie said: I definitely agree with you John.

Marie asked: John, does your wife work?

John replied: oh yes, she is a journalist!

Marie said; oh wonderful. I work at the office. You know how hard it is when you have children. Larsen is always too busy with his work and so do I. we are not spending too much time together as a couple. Larsen added: don't worry dear, we are going to have some time together. 'They spent a wonderful evening at the Larson house.'

John said: thank you for the lovely dinner Marie. It was wonderful.

Marie replied: It was my pleasure and very nice to meet you John.

Larsen added; I shall see you tomorrow at the office.

John added: thank you. Good night to you both!'

'John has left the Larson house.'

'John has spent more time looking at the pictures of the crime scene. He was trying to find more evidence that will prove that the killer is Jules.

Jules has been killing innocent women for almost a decade. And he still hasn't been caught.

'John has been sure that something important is missing in this case, that something is not very clear.' 'The following day John was very early in the office.' Larsen asked: hey John how are you? Any news?

John added: hey, I have been looking at the pictures of the crime scene. I'm sure something is not ok in this case.

Larsen asked: what is not ok?

John said: I have got a strange feeling about these murders. Maybe we are chasing the wrong guy!'

Larsen asked: what makes you think that?

John said: I think we should try to find the real mother from Julian and Jules. If she is still alive. It is worth a try.'

Larsen added: ok I will do some research now!

John added: yes do now so we can go and talk to her .Of course if she is alive. I don't think that Julian knows much about his real mother; he was adopted from birth. If we can find her she can help us a lot in this case. As I said before we may be missing an important detail. Larsen said: ok John.

'After a couple of hours Larsen has found her. She was still alive and she was at the nursing home.' 'Larsen knocks at the door.'

Larsen said: hey John I found her, let's go.

John added: excellent job. Let's go/

John asked: do you think we should say to Julian?

Larsen said: oh no. I don't think that is a good idea!"

John replied: ok.

"Arriving at the place, detectives were looking for Mrs Luis." Larsen asked : Good day nurse we would like to speak to Mrs Luis! John asked: can we talk to her? It won't take long!? Nurse replied; yes of course follow me please.

Nurse opened the door and said: hi Mrs Louis you have company today.

' She was looking very old and drained.'

Luis asked: who are these people? What do they want ?

'The first came John.'

John said; we are from the police. We would like to ask you a few questions about your sons Jules and Julian!

Luis asked: what do I want to know about my two sons?

Larsen added: listen please ! What can you tell us about your son Jules? It is very important!

Luis said: my son Jules died a very long time ago. He hangs himself . Me and my Joe found him. Also I have my Julian, the other son he has been adopted . I give my own son away. I hope he is well. 'John and Larsen couldn't believe it .'

John said: what a fuck man!

Larsen said: thank you Mrs Luis .

' They left the room . They didn't know what was going on and who was the real killer.' 'They went back to the police station.'

Larsen said: I think we should tell Julian.

John added: I don't understand! Who is the killer?

Larsen added: something is missing in this case!

John added: I'm going to call Julian now!

' He closes the door and walks down the corridor.'

'The phone rang."

John said: hi Julian. How are you?

Julian responded: hi detective any news?

John asked: could you come today to the police station?

Julian replied: oh no, I can't. I'm busy. I have to call my wife later on. Soon I will be going back to Spain!

John added: Julian your brother he is not the killer. Today we have spoken to your real mother. She told us that your twin brother Jules had hung himself a very long time ago. 'Julian was very quiet.'

John asked again: Julian are you there?

Julian responded: Oh my god. My mother, you met my real mother? What? My brother has died?

John responded: I'm very sorry Julian.

Julian said: oh this is all very confusing for me. I will be leaving soon! I would like to know who has broken into my apartment?

John said: this is leading us to investigate. Probably the killer I would say. Well I wish you safe back home Julian and thank you very much for the collaboration with us. Julian said: thank you for the information you gave me.'

John said: Bye-bye Julian.

Julian replied: bye detective.

'John walks to Larsen's office.'

John said: hey ,I just spoke to Julian. I told him everything. He will be going back to Spain.

John added: this all stinks, it's not right!

John asked, "Where is Anne?

Larsen asked: what do you want to know, where is Anne? She took a couple of days off!

John asked: what do you know about her?

Larsen responded; hmm not very much. She works here for a couple of months!

' Hold on, do you think that Anne is a killer? John added: she can be !!

John said: check everything about Anne. It's very important! I will try to call Julian one more time. 'Julian has been packing , he is ready to go home. He had a strange feeling.

'He just left the hotel .'

'Detective John couldn't reach him on the phone ."

'Two hours later Larset had a file about Anne. What he discovered was shocking. He urgently called the Spanish police .'

'John entered the room.'

John said: I couldn't reach Julian. He must have gone to the airport.

John asked: what have you got about Anne?

Larsen said: you were right about Anne! ' Anne or Marcus Mcallister are the same person. He is the killer! He did some plastic surgery on his face because he wanted to look like a woman.

He even changed his voice! What is shocking about Marcus, he has been abused as a child from his own mother. He set up Julian and Jules. And of course as she was a part of the police she knew everything. I have already contacted the police in Spain as I think she or he will try to kill Julians family. 'John has been in shock.'

John added; I hope we did react on time. I hope it's not too late!

'The sun was coming down in Spain.' Katharine was putting her children to bed when someone knocked at the door.

'She was thinking it must be someone from the police. Maybe they need something.' 'Katharine opened the door .In front of her stood the woman.'

Katharine asked: who are you? Can I help you?

Anne said; oh good evening . My name is Anee. I.m new detective. I.m here to protect your family. Anne said; May I use your restroom please, hm I really need it !

'Katharine was looking around, she couldn't see any of the police officers.' Katharine said: yes please. The toilet is just down the corridor then left! Anee replied: thank you very much!

'While Kathrine was cleaning the kitchen , Anne approached her from the back.' 'She grabs Katharine for the hair and stabs her two times in the back.' 'Katharine screams.' help, help me"'

'Katharine was fighting for her life.'She fell down on the kitchen floor.' 'The last thing in her mind was her husband Julian and the children.'

Anne or Marcus was standing there watching poor Katharine fighting for her life.'

'Marxus said: you fucking butch you will die tonight. Nobody will save you,ha,ha. I killed more than 20 women like you. The women like you do not deserve to live, they deserve to die. I set up everything for your dear husband. The police think that Julian's twin brother is the killer. I'm the killer.'

' Marcus was preparing to rape her and finish the ritual.'

Katharine was lying on the floor and she was bleeding heavily.

'Julian was waiting for the taxi at the airport.'he couldn't wait to see her wife and children.' 'Marcus was getting ready to finish his ritual when he heard police cars.; 'He pulls out from his pocket a gun.'

'The police cars were everywhere around the house . Police have broken down the door and entered inside the house.they could see Katharine lying on the floor bleeding heavily.The ambulance car was on its way.

'Marcus was hiding behind the door holding a gun.'

'Police were shouted: check the house, he must be hiding somewhere inside!

One policeman went to check the first floor when Marcus attacked him from behind.

'They were fighting on the floor. The police officer pulls the trigger out and shoots Marcus a couple of times.'

'Marcus was finally dead.

'The rest of the team came up and saw the dead Marcus lying on the floor.

'Julian has just arrived. He saw his wife Katharine fighting for her life. The children were fine but still in shock.'

'After a couple of days detective John has called Julian.'

John asked: How are you Julian? How is your wife?

Julian replied: Thank you for sending the police over here. I'm happy that this is over . My wife will make it!'

'Sitting in the darkroom watching the rain falling down, holding a glass of brandy in his left hand and the cigar in his right hand, John Coleman was focusing on his new case.'

It was late at night, and his wife was already in a deep sleep. You could hear the car's noise down the road.'

His big apartment was on the E50 Madison Av. He was living there all his life with his wife Julia.

John was looking at the pictures of two dead bodies, both males around '40s.

Police found the bodies down the Bronx river laying down on the wet grass covered in blood.

'Coleman noticed both victims were missing one finger on the left-hand side'.

He knew this time he was dealing with the serial killer.

'These murders were somehow different from the previous cases he was dealing with!.'

He put his hand down the table smoking his last cigar.' Resting in his chair.'

'His new colleague is a very young detective by the name Edward Collins.'

Coleman knew to work with Edward on this case. It's not going to be easy. He is a young man not very experienced and very impulsive.'

'Analysis of the dead bodies from the pictures Coleman started to concentrate on the killer profile.'

There were a lot of things to work out in this case.

It was coming very late. He dropped the file on the table below preparing himself for a late sleep.

'He thought to himself:' ' Another murder to resolve.'

It was coming at 7 am. His wife Julia has prepared strong coffee and went to wake up her husband.'

Opening the bedroom door she heard the noise from the shower, she knew that John was already awake. She went back to the kitchen to make some fresh toast and eggs.

'John has entered the kitchen.' he said:'

'Good morning my darling.! The food smells delicious.'

Julia responded:' Oh my love, thanks! I guess you were up late last night, do you want to talk about it?' she asked:'

Coleman murmured:' hm! Yes, I have been working on the new case! It looks like we have a serial killer this time to deal with.'!

Julia stretched her hair, she looked at him with her eyes wide open!' she added:'

Oh dear, I'm sorry to hear that!'

John asked:' Anyway, what are you doing today? Any plans?

She responded: Hmm yes I need to go to my office. I have a busy day today!'

Coleman responded;' Oh my love, me too. I will finish my coffee and I have to run! I don't know when I will be back. You know how It is with my job!'

'He comes closer and kisses her very intensively. I love you, Julia'

'He closes the door behind him holding in one hand cups of coffee and on the other hand an egg sandwich.'

He has to be on time at the police station.'

Traffic was so busy as usual, New York is a busy town.' 'Coleman thought to himself.'

'He knew there was a lot of work to do!

' Coleman has put his one hand in his left pocket taking one cigar. He was getting closer to his workplace .'

'As usual, he was looking to find a place to park his car.' It was always the same problem in New York. City.'

Driving around looking for a parking space he finally managed to find the space where to park his car. He quickly locked the door from the car rushing to his workplace. It was getting to 8 am.'

'Arriving at the police station his boss Mike has called him to come into his office immediately.'

'Coleman could see that Edward, his new colleague, was already there!'

'He opens the door.' He said;'

Hey Mike whats up, Hi Edward!'

'Mike has been looking very stressed. His face was looking very irritated somehow.'

'Coleman noticed at first.'

'Mike has puffing cigar:' he said:'

'Where the hell have you been John, you are late!'

"We have so far two murder, both males around 40'!'

'John eyebrows went up:' he responded in a casual tone.'

'Sorry Mike, I was working last night on our case and this morning I got stuck in the traffic.'

As I can see from the pictures both males are missing one finger on the left-hand side.'

What I'm trying to say here, is that we are dealing with a serial killer.' Coleman added.'

Mike responded;' I know that Coleman already! The thing is we have to catch this person, which means we have a lot of work to do!' I would send you and Edward today to the crime scene down the Bronx. The forensic team couldn't find anything so far.!'

'Mike was furious.'

'Coleman murmured to himself;' He responded'

Ok, Mike no problem! Me and Edward we are going now on the Crime scene to check if we can discover something which will take us to resolve these murders.'

'Edward was observing all the conversation between Coleman and Mike.'

'Coleman has noticed that Mike has changed a lot after his wife died in a car accident 3 months ago,'

'Edward and Coleman have left the office and driven to the Bronx.'

'Coleman said:'

Hey Edward, did you hear how he was talking to me.?'

``I think our boss Mike has changed a lot lately.'

Edward puffed his cigar concentrated on the drive.ahead!

Edward responded:'

Yea, well I'm new here, I'm only two months working here so I don't know Mike so well, but you know him very well I guess!'

'Coleman has lit his cigar .' He said;'

Yes I know Mike for a very long time, he was a very jolly person but since his wife died he has changed a lot.'

Something has changed in him.' 'Coleman added:'

'Edward said:'

Ah well, I guess It's not easy when you lose your loved one. We can all change at this point. We are not the same person as we were before.'

Coleman has smiled;' he added:

'Very true Edward.'

'Coleman asked;' What about you Edward? Are you married? Any brothers and sisters?

'Edward answered Coleman:' Well I'm not married yet! I do have a girlfriend Susan.

My parents live in San Francisco and I'm an only child .'

'Coleman puffed cigar intensively;'

He added:' Ah so you are an only child! That's interesting!'

'They came to the Bronx.'

'Edward stopped the car.'

'Both detectives went out to look around the river in the hope to find some evidence.'

'You could see the blood of the dead bodies covering the grass."

'Coleman went on one side of the river and Edward on the other part of the river.'

'Coleman was observing every single detail on the floor, he went a couple of times around and down on the bottom of the river something very shiny had caught his eye.

'He quickly moved down the river and what he saw was a shiny working pen.

'He picked up the item and he added the Item into the plastic bag.'

'Coleman was hoping he will find the fingerprints on the pen

'He didn't want to tell Edward anything .'

'They spend a few hours down the Bronx.'

'Edward come back' he asked;'

Hey, Coleman, any news?

'Coleman murmured;' Hmm nothing yet!

How about you?' John asked.'

Edward responded:' Nothing. I look around but there is nothing here.' A forensic team has been here and they couldn't find anything except the dead bodies.' What the hell Coleman!'

"You okay?" Coleman asked;'

Edward responded;' Yea I'm ok! Moving quickly to the car to grab his cup of coffee.'

'Coleman has received a phone call.'

It was Mike on the other line saying there were found two more dead bodies this time very close to the Swan River.' Mike has ordered Coleman and Edward to go immediately over there.'

Coleman put his phone down and said:' Mike just phone me up!'

Hey, Edward, we have got two more dead bodies close to the Swan River!'

'Come on we have to go!'

'Edward said;' What the hell" two more dead bodies?

Coleman eyebrows went up.' Don't ask! We have to go now!'

'Edward said:' No problem man, we are going!' As I can see we will have two more dead bodies!' This is crazy!' He added:'

'Coleman was checking his pockets. He wanted to be sure the little item found on the floor was in his pocket.' He was looking out of the window and thinking about how he will get a fingerprint very soon.'

Coleman said:' I know how this sounds to you but yes we will have every one week two more dead bodies. We are dealing with a serial killer and It's never easy to catch them.'

I know that from my own experience working all my life in this department.'

'Edward responded:' Yes I know! I wish to catch this psycho soon.'

Coleman said:' Take it easy! This is just the beginning!' We have a lot of work to do.'

``John has been thinking why the killer is killing just a man. He wanted to investigate more about these men. Somehow he hadn't been sure whether there was a serial killer involved or we were dealing with the mafia.' He found this case very strange.' For the first time in his career, he wasn't completely sure.'

'Edward looked at him and asked:'

Hey, Coleman, you are looking like you are in deep thoughts.'

What's wrong man?' Edward asked;'

'Coleman droped cigar down the ashtray:' He responded in casual tone voice;"

Nothing is wrong, I'm just thinking about these murders.'

'Hmm said Edward:'

'They stopped the car.' There were a lot of people around, a forensic team was there.too.

'Coleman came first.' He was observing the bodies.' Same everything.'

Both males again, missing the finger on the left-hand side.'

'Edward was talking to the people trying to collect as much more information:"

'One girl was standing over there, she was looking terrified.'

'Coleman came closer to the girl,' He was holding his hands inside the pocket. His body movements were very slow."

'He looked at her then asked:'

I would like to ask you a couple of questions.' said Coleman.'

'The girl looked at him.' She was shocked that she couldn't speak for some reason.' The way she looked scared of her own shadow! I've never seen a woman look so frightened...

'Then she spoke,'

What would you like to know about detectives?' she asked.'

Coleman scratches his eyebrow.' He asked;'

Did you call the police?

'The girl has been looking very confused and scared.'

She said:' Yes detective. I was walking around with my dog today when I discovered the bodies.' I called the straightaway police.'

'Coleman asked again.'

Did you notice someone around this area? Men or maybe women? Did you see anyone?

'Girl was quiet for a minute or two then she added:'

I think I did!'

'Coleman reacted impulsively he asked:' What do you mean you think you did! Who was it? men or women?' Please, can you remember we are trying to catch this person, you must tell me!!!'

'The girl has murmured:' She asked:'

'Please do you have one cigarette for me?'

'Coleman said:' Yes of course! Wait here!

'He went to Edward's car to take a packet of cigarettes.' When he came back the girl was gone. She disappeared.'

'Oh shit now I will have to chase a bloody girl,' Said John .'

'He went back to Edward.' He added:'

Let's go! I witnessed the young girl but she didn't want to collaborate and she had a bloody runoff.'

I suggest we go back to the police station. I found this girl and I think she saw what happened.'

Edward added:' Ok, let's go!'

'Edward asked:' why did she run off?

'Coleman responded:' I guess she got scared but we will find her!.'

'Coleman was puffing his cigar;he scratched his feet sitting very comfortably in the car.'

He added:' Oh I'm damn tired of chasing the killer. I'm getting older.' All my life I dedicated myself to serving the police and now I'm getting so tired.' Soon I will retire from this job.'

'Edward was laughing.' He said: Come on man. You are still in good shape, you don't want to retire yet! I know you are one of the best detectives.'

'Coleman murmured;' Yes I'm but sometimes It's really hard. This job is keeping you away from your dear family. you are always so busy that sometimes you forget that you have a home and the wife waiting for you at home."

Edward added:' I know that that's why I don't want to get married yet! I have this girlfriend Susan. I told you about her. We have been together for 4 years but I'm still not ready to commit.' Apart from my job I would like to enjoy my job and my freedom.'

Coleman said;' Yeah, that's a good idea!'

'Edward has stopped the car in front of the police station.'

'Both detectives went inside."

'Coleman has noticed Mike wasn't there in his office."'

He sat in his chair and grabbed a cup of coffee, trying to find a girl who had run away from the crime scene.

'He spends hours looking for information about the girl." and he finally got her address and phone number. Luckily he has got her name from the forensic team because she was talking to them first.

'Coleman knew where she was living.'

He decided to go there alone.'

'He took the car key from Edward and drove off.'

'She was living in Manhattan.' Not too far. 'Coleman thought to himself.'

'Driving fast he managed to find the perfect parking space.

'He just finished smoking his cigar as always and took the stairs up to the Melanie apartment.'

'Coleman could hear the noise inside the apartment.'

'He rang twice.'

'Someone was coming to open the door.'

'When she recognized the detective she tried to close the door but Coleman was quicker.'

'She said with a very upsetting tone in her voice;'

'How did you find me, detective!? What do you want from me?'

'Coleman was looking at her.'

He added:' Listen, Miss! You ran off this morning from the crime scene! The forensic team has given me your name and the rest was easy.'

I would like to ask you a couple of questions!

I'm working on this case and for me, It's only important to resolve this case nothing else!.

Now I would like to ask you why did you run off?

'The woman was staring at him.' She took a glass of brandy and she offered it to him.'

'Coleman has refused to drink on his duty.'

She set on the sofa bed took a deep breath and said:'

'Well I was walking my dog this morning. We went close to the river where I discovered the two dead bodies. I was looking around and I think I saw a woman running off. She was wearing a black suit. She didn't look very tall. Black hair, extremely black hair she had.'

'Melanie was puffing the cigar.'

'She didn't see me, I'm sure she didn't.' This is all the detective.'

'Coleman was listening very carefully."

'Coleman's eyebrows went up; he said:

Thank you, Melanie. I would like to ask you one more question.'

Did you see her face? Or just you saw this woman from behind? Is she young? Older?

Is she black or white? Every detail is very important."

Please try to remember!'

'Melanie stood up;' She was looking out of the window holding the glass of brandy.'

She said:' To me, she was looking white, as I said before she was wearing a black suit and she wasn't that tall.' All of this I already described to the forensic team before you came, detective.'

'Coleman added:'

No problem Melanie and thank you very much. You have been very helpful.'

You shouldn't run this morning.' he added;"

'She said:' I hope this woman didn't see me!!'

'Coleman has turned around and said: Well If you are scared or not sure if this woman saw you or not we can provide you with the security if you want?' he said;"

'She added;' Detective it would be good if you can give me your phone number in case I change my mind.'

Coleman has pulled from his right pocket the detective card and given it to her.'

'He turns around ready to go.'

He said;' Thank you again for your collaboration and if you need something called me in my office the number is there.'

She responded:' Yes detective.'

'Coleman has left her apartment and now he has got more information about who can be the killer.'

'Driving back to the police station, his phone rang."

'Coleman has pulled off on the side of the road and answered the phone:'

'He could see his boss Mike was trying to reach him.'

He answered the phone;'

Hey Mike is everything ok? Coleman asked:'

Mike responded with an angry tone of voice:' where are you, John?

Coleman responded:' I was doing my job, Mike. I went to ask a witness a couple of questions.'

Mike added:' what witness?

'Coleman said: Can we talk when I get back? It takes a long time.'

'Mike was sitting in his chair in the office drinking his coffee.'

Mike said:' Ok John. Hurry up!!.' See you soon!'

'Coleman had a strange feeling about Mike.' He wanted to investigate a little more about Mike's wife and how she died.' He knew Mike for a very long time working with him and he found his behavior very strange.'

'He knew now he had one witness and he got a golden pen. found on the Bronx River.

He was needing more evidence.' he knew that.'

Driving back to office he was in deep thoughts.'

'Coleman has stopped the car very close to the office.'

He crossed the street to buy his late lunch and a cup of coffee.

He sat on the bench eating his freshly made sandwich in peace before he went back to the office trying to understand the killer's mind.' why all the dead men were in the early '40s.

'Why are they missing one finger on the left-hand side?'

'Checking the man's profile Coleman discovered that all the men that have been murdered so far all had a good job and very rich lifestyle.'

'That doesn't make any sense to me.' I think this has nothing to do with a serial killer.'

'He thought to himself.'

'The next important thing is to send that golden pencil for analysis. Coleman was hoping he would have those fingerprints very soon.'

'Arriving at his office Mike was waiting for him.'

'Coleman went straight away to Mike's office which was located down the corridor on the left side.'

He knocks on the door first then opens the door of the Mike office.'

'Mike was sitting there in his chair, he was talking to someone on the phone, he pointed at me with his finger to sit down.'

'Mike has put his phone down and said:' where have you been John? We have got a lot of work to do! I was waiting for you!' you always disappear when I need you here."

'Coleman responded in his casual tone voice:"

Well, Mike, as I told you I was doing my job man!'

I went to see this witness Melanie, she discovered the bodies this morning.

She said that she saw the woman running off from the crime scene this morning.

'Mike face turns into a hot red.'

He replied:' What the hell are you talking about Coleman. What witness?

I spoke to the forensic team this morning and they didn't say anything about any women.'

Mike stood up from his chair, very irritated .'

Coleman asked:' What is wrong with you Mike, do you have some problems. I must say I have known you for a very long time and this is not you man!!'

What is going on Mike!' Coleman asked;'

'Mike responded; Nothing is wrong. Sometimes I just find it very hard for this job.

After my wife died, it was not easy.' I have one daughter and she is not very good at school. she is giving it to me.' I don't know what to do with her.'

'Mike was holding his hands in his pockets.'

'Coleman murmured:' Sorry to hear that. I know It's not easy to do this job but we have to.

Private life should be left at home. I do understand you, Mike.' I'm getting very tired but we do need to resolve these murders and this is our job.'

Coleman asked:' Where is Edward?'

Mike said;' He is in his office working.'

'Mike asked:' So who is this witness?

'Coleman has puffed his cigar:' He added:'

'She is a very young girl I would say nearly in her20s. She discovered the dead bodies and she called the police. She is convinced that she saw the women with the black hair running away from the crime scene. Melanie did say that she is not sure if the woman has seen her."

Mike added:' Oh so we could have a woman serial killer is that what you are trying to say?'

'Coleman said:" So far we have one witness. Every week we will find two dead bodies in different parts of New York. So the next murder It will probably happen sometime next week.'

'Mike was very pale.'

Mike added:' Ok Coleman I will leave it to you and Edward to do the job.'

I'm going home now. I have to pick up my daughter from school, so I will see you tomorrow in the office. If anything happens, just give me a call,"

'Coleman has stood up from the chair: he said:

No problem Mike. Go and have a rest!' See you tomorrow."

'Leaving Mike's office Coleman went to see Edward."

'Hey, Edward!' John asked" How is your work going?

Hi John" where have you been? I have been to your office but you haven't been there!?'

'Edward asked."

'Coleman responded:' I went to talk to that girl this morning.'

'Coleman added:';' Very interesting news I've got.' Apparently what the girl said the killer is the woman with the black hair and she is not very tall.' Age around maybe early '30s.

'Edward was looking surprised;' he added:" well done John.' Now, at last, we have something."

Coleman responded in a very low tone of voice:' I hope that we will soon find our answers and catch this woman.'

'Edward said:' Yes, me too. I worked on the file all afternoon. I found out that all the men we have found dead so far there are pretty much all from the rich families. So I found this weird.'

'Coleman took a deep breath and responded:' Yes I know Edward. I have been looking at the same thing before I went to speak to the girl Melanie this afternoon.'

'It doesn't make sense.'

'Edward responded:' we will see what is going on behind all of this.'

Coleman asked:' Did you have your lunch? If you didn't go ahead. you have a break for 30 min.' Mike went home a long time ago.' he is not in his office.' John added;"

Edward said:' Thanks, John. I will take a break now.' See you later!'

'Coleman has shut the door behind and gone back into his office.'

'His wife Julian has left him a message.'

'Hi, love, hope your job is going well.' I will come late tonight. I'm going with my friends for a drink.'

'See you at home. Love Julian.'

'John was trying to figure out all about these murders. He was working until 9 pm. Edward had gone home, only Coleman was still in his office. He decided to go home. He was needing a rest. He stood up from his chair and closed the door behind him. It was a heatwave all day. Summer was doing the best this year. 'Coleman has thought to himself."

'Driving back home John was thinking about his wife Julian. He couldn't wait to arrive at home.'

'He left the car close to his house.' Claiming the stairs very slowly he was feeling very tired.

He finally managed to reach the apartment. He opens the door living his jacket and the keys on the table below."

Coleman has noticed that his wife is not yet at home. He thought to himself" Probably she will come back later.' He sat down on his sofa bed putting the tv on and having a glass of brandy.'

'As he felt so tired he slept on the sofa bed.'

He woke up around 6 am he went to the bedroom to wake up his wife."

"Opening the bedroom door Julia wasn't there!"

'What is going on.' He shouted,' he couldn't believe it.'

Coleman went straightaway to check his mobile phone and the house phone.' He knew Julia wouldn't do something like that never.' He was feeling something had happened to his wife.'

'On the mobile phone there were no messages but on the house phone it was.'

'Your wife has been kidnapped you will have to do what I'm saying or she will be dead very soon."

'It was a very deep voice, but not like the human voice.'

'Coleman was trying to keep calm. He dresses very quickly and runs to his office.'

'He was driving fast to his job. He knew somehow all of this was connected with his job.

Someone was trying to set him up. Someone who was very afraid that the real truth will be discovered soon." Someone who is killing those innocent men."

'He was keeping his mobile phone on all the time in case the killer phoned him up.'

Arriving at the police station at his office nobody wasn't there. It was still very early.'

'Stressing out want help;" He thought to himself."

He grabs a cup of coffee and he sits down in his chair.' Coleman was waiting for Edward to turn up and Mike."

'It was coming at 8 am .' 'Coleman could hear some noise down the corridor he opens the door from his office and Edward was there just entering in his office when Coleman said;'

'Edward please can you come over here I need to talk to you."

Edward said; Hey John, you are already here.'

'Edward has noticed something was wrong just by looking at the expression on John's face.'

He asked:' what is going on John? Are you alright?'

'Coleman has shut the door from his office." He said:

'I have got to tell you something Edward.' You have to keep it for yourself please.!' It is very important.'

Edward was looking at his eyes.' His eyes were infuriated and very worried.' Coleman's face was hot red.' Edward knew something has happened."

``Coleman said in a very low voice" Last night my wife was kidnapped.' I have got the message left at my house phone. I do suspect what is going on. But at this moment I can not do much expect to wait for the phone call."

'Edward's face turned pale.' he asked," Who could do that ?' Why is your wife?

Coleman scratches his hair;" he responds casually." As I said I do suspect who is standing behind all of this but I need a piece of strong evidence. I will ask you as your colleague and friend you must keep very quiet until I prove who is the killer.' Did you hear me, Edward? Not even one single word to Mike!'

Edward murmured:' Ok John no problem I will keep quiet, but you have to find your wife."

Edward asked:' But what do they want from your wife? Money? Or something else?

Coleman said;' I think they wanted me to give up from this case."

Edward was looking very confused.' He added; What? They want you to give up on this case!

But why? What is going on?

Coleman answered.' Don't ask me questions, Edward. I already told you I suspect what is going on but I have to prove it. We will continue to work on this case together. And I hope my wife will make it. This is a big shock for me Edward.'

Edward puffed the cigar. He added:' Ok Coleman. I'm going back to my office. If you need anything, let me know.

Coleman said dubiously: Thanks, Edward. See you later.'

``John has noticed that Mike didn't come to work. He decided to phone him up on his home phone.'

While he was trying to reach Mike. Edward has entered Coleman's office saying it was another murder. But this time the woman died.'

Coleman has put his phone down. He felt so stressed. Not knowing is going to see his wife dead.'

John was holding his cigar in his right hand. He said:

'Let's go, Edward.' There is no time to waste.' Coleman was checking his mobile phone all the time but still nothing, not a word ."

He asked Edward: So where are we going?

Edward responded: I'm sorry but that girl Melanie was murdered early this morning in her apartment.' The girl who was our witness!'

'Coleman as soon as he heard he knew deep down what was going on. He still didn't have time to send that golden pen for the analysis but he was hoping to do it today.' He had to act very quickly. Coleman thought to himself: 'The woman assassin who is working for someone trying to set me up by kidnapping my wife.'

'Edward has driven fast to Manhattan.' Arriving at the crime scene Melanie was lying on the kitchen floor covered in blood. She was shot in the had."

'Coleman investigated the crime scene and somehow he knew deep down that this was a setup. There is no serial killer involved something much more was going on."

Edward went across the hall into the bedroom of Miss Melanie checking and collecting the fingerprints.

Edward said sharply:" There is nothing here Coleman!' I went to speak with some of Melanie's neighbors but they didn't hear anything'. People they quiet in shock. They liked Melanie as a person."

'Coleman was staring at the dead woman's face lying on the kitchen floor."

John added in a low tone voice:" We have to keep working."

Edward said with understanding:" Oh man I'm sorry about your wife! I hope you will find her no matter what!"

Coleman's face went pale and he responded: Let's go!

Coleman added:' By the way, what looks like someone has opened the Melanie door and he shot her straightaway in the head. There were no signs of any violence involved. We will see when the autopsy has been done maybe then we will know more." At least she didn't miss any fingers."

'True enough, John."

Edward said suddenly:"

'There was a minute of silence between two detectives.:'

You're very silent, John" said Edward."

John murmured.' he added:' Listen Edward I will take you to the police station and I'm going home for a while. There is no Mike today in the office.' If you need me you can give me a call. Is that ok? John asked:"

Edward replied in the low tone voice:' No problem John. I still have to finish my work for today"

'Edward was puffing cigar."

'Coleman has left Edward in front of the Police station. His thoughts were with Julian all the time. Trying to resolve these cases he felt like he was chasing ghosts." The first time in his life he felt confused, maybe because this time was missing his wife. But he will never give up." He thought." I will resolve this case no matter what." I will catch the killer.'

'On the way home, he stopped to buy some food.' What he saw was very impressive. He saw the daughter. The girl was standing there smoking a cigarette. She was wearing very dirty clothes. It looked like she's waiting for someone to turn up. 'Coleman was observing her for a while then he decided to approach her."

'He came closer to her." he said:' Hi Nicole how are you? What are you doing here?

'She looked at him with the eyes open like she saw the ghost in front of her. With one hand she gently scratched her ear:' she responded;' Oh hello Mr Coleman! I was just waiting for my dad to come and pick me up, he didn't go today at work. I don't know why he is so late?!"

' Coleman thought she was looking very messy."

Coleman said quickly" Can I ask you something Nickole?'

Nicole responded:" Yes Mr Coleman what would you like to know?"

'Coleman puffed smoke in the air." he asked:" Do you know why your dad didn't show up today at his work? Is there anything unusual happening lately with your dad?

Nicole responded quickly:" Oh yeah my dad has become very strange after my mom died in the car accident.' He is always going all the time somewhere on his own. I tried to ask him a couple of times but he always responds to me the same. So I guess I just gave up. I hope he will be better."

Oh look he did send one of our neighbors to pick me up;" bye Mr Coleman I gotta go now. It was nice to talk to you. Bye."

Coleman added: Bye Nickole. Take care."

Walking to his car Coleman was thinking about the conversation with Nicole. He knew that something wasn't right with Mike.' He was trying to find out."

'He wanted to get home in case he had any news about his missing wife.' he was so worried."

He was stuck in the traffic for the last hour on the way home.' He couldn't find the soft spot or the quiet place in his mind but he tried."

'But I confess no matter what I did, I couldn't stop thinking about my wife Julia."

He finally has reached his apartment. He opens the door, at first he didn't notice but then he saw a white envelope on the floor. He felt like somebody was in his apartment."

He picked up the envelope and sat on the sofa bed to read it."

' Mr Coleman if you don't drop this case your wife soon she will die." we are watching over you."

'His face turns into the hot red by reading those words." He didn't feel scared but he was worried for his wife Julia."

He decided to send this letter together with the shiny pencil to the lab for analysis. He knew something mast came up." A part that he was suspecting what was going on, he needed a piece of very strong evidence to prove it."

'Later that night he rang up to his old friend Andrew who was working in the lab analysis."

'Andrew was his best friend. John knew he could count on him no matter what."

"Coleman's detective instincts told him there would be something interesting behind all of this."

'That night everything was arranged.'

'Lying in the darkroom he was trying to get some sleep. The air was extremely hot he could feel his body was sweating." He opened the window to let some fresh air inside the room."

His deep thoughts were with Julian. He was hoping that soon he will find her."

'The early sunlight coming into the room Coleman woke up. He thought to himself: Must be very early.

He got up, looking at his watch on the little table below. It was 5 am.

He dresses, going into the kitchen to prepare the coffee and something to eat.

He couldn't stop thinking about his wife."

'He knew he had to continue on this case no matter what."

'He prepared everything to send the items to the analysis before he goes to work."

'It will take one week to get the result." 'John has thought."

'Coleman was ready to live his apartment when the house phone rang."

His body started to tremble in fear that he would hear bad news about his wife Julian.'

'Hello, who is this? John asked:'

Hey John, It's me, Edward!' How are you?

Oh hi, Edward, any news? John asked:

Edward said: We have two more dead bodies both males. Down in Manhattan.' I will come to pick you up. Be ready in 20 min."

John has puffed the smoke in the air: He responded:" I'm ready."

'Opening the door from his apartment cool air rushed towards him as he went down the stairs."

'While he was waiting for Edward to turn up he managed to send the two items in the lab for analysis."

'Trying to connect all the puzzles to resolve this mysterious case he knew he was getting closer and closer."

'Edward has just arrived.' He saw John waiting on the corner, and he stopped the car.'

He said:' Good morning John.' How are you? Hey John, nice spot you've found for yourself while you were waiting for me.' I hope you didn't wait long!!' Mike our boss has gone for a holiday break I heard this morning in the office."

'Coleman has cast a quick look over his shoulder." he added:' There is so little time left to resolve this case. We have to act quickly Edward." He puffed his cigar in the air: '' He said;

It doesn't surprise me that Mike has taken his holiday."

Edward's eyes opened very wide: he asked; ``What do you mean by that Coleman?' Any news about your missing wife?"

Coleman added:" Nothing yet about my wife Julian." So we have two more dead bodies down in Manhattan?"

'Edward murmured:' Hm, yes." I worked yesterday in the office. Something important is missing in this case." I can't figure it out yet but I'm working on it."

'Coleman reflected for a minute." then he said;"

'Hm, that's what I'm thinking as well."

'They were driving towards Manhattan at the crime scene."

'Arriving down the Hudson river two dead bodies were lying on the floor covered in blood.' Coleman looked around."

'With a quick movement, Edward was beside him."

'He said:" "There is something very strange about all this." I Can't figure it out!"

'Coleman added:" We will now proceed to the next stage of our investigation."

'Our forensic team will to the rest." We don't have any witnesses!' To me, these murders are very well planned."

'Edward stared at him."

He asked:" Are you sure?

' Coleman responded doubtfully:" Yes I'm sure but we have to prove it."

'Edward paused and then went on:" I think we should go back to the office. As I said before our Mike has gone on holiday and we are here struggling to resolve this case. What a hell he thinks." Edward shouted;"

'Coleman said:" Oh I agree with you." Take it easy."

'Coleman was waiting for the results to come up from the lab." he was pretty confident as always. He knew this case soon will be over."

He remembered the conversation with Nicole and he wanted to investigate more about Mike's wife and how she died."

'Later that day he left Edward in front of the Police station."

``During the investigation, Coleman was very much interested in one particular man who was murdered." His name was Alan Peterson.' One of the victims.'"

``Alan has lived in Manhattan with his wife Susan." They didn't have any children."

'Coleman has stopped the car in front of Alan's house."

'Coleman looked around."

'He thought to himself'. What a wonderfully peaceful spot." 'He rang twice at ring bell."

'In front of him appeared Middle age women.'

'He started when he saw her:" Hello, I'm Detective John Coleman. I would like to ask you a couple of questions about your husband Alan?"

'Susan replied pleasantly." Hi Detective. My name is Susan please come on in."

She asked:' Can I get you something, tea or coffee perhaps?'

'Coleman responded gently." Coffee would be fine, thank you."

'She came back after a couple of minutes."

'She sat down beside him." She asked:' What would you like to know about my husband?'

'Coleman puffed his cigar in the air.' he asked:" Can you tell me is it your husband Alan was behaving strangely lately before he was murdered? Have you noticed something unusual in your marriage?

Susan studs up and took a step forward." she responded slowly:" Hm, good question Detective!'

'She took a deep breath then she added:" I believe my husband was having an affair."

'I did suspect for quite a while." He was refusing lately to not have any intimacy involved with me."

'You know what I mean detective? She asked:"

'Coleman said in a low voice." Oh, I'm sorry to hear that. It must be very painful for you as a woman to discover something like that?"

Coleman asked:" Have you ever tried to find out about these other women?'

Susan said in lower voice tone:" Maybe I will disappoint you detective but the fact is I never

tried to find out who the woman my husband was seeing.' I knew deep down that he is in a relationship with somebody else but somehow I wanted to save our marriage if you understand what I'm saying."

'Coleman said quickly;" Oh I do understand you, Mrs Susan."

He asked:' Do you know when this affair started? When has your husband changed?

'There was a pause." then Susan said:"

Oh, It's hard to say! I believe this affair went on for a couple of months or maybe more I'm not so sure."

'I would like to ask you, Detective.' She asked:'

'Coleman responded." Yes, of course, Mrs." What would you like to know?"

'Susan sat down." she asked:" Have you caught the killer yet??

'He paused and looked around." he responded:" Unfortunately not yet but we are working on it."

'Susan added:" Well, what more can I say? I wish you all well with your work detective."

'Coleman has stood up following the corridor to the main door."

'He added: Thank you for your time, Susan. You have been very helpful."

'She looked at him with shining eyes.' she said:" Bye detective."

'After the conversation with Mrs, Susan Coleman has driven off to the center of Manhattan."

'He wanted to spend some time alone analyzing this case. He decided to go to a good restaurant for a meal."

'His deep thoughts were with his wife Julia." He was hoping to find her soon."

'He stopped the car in front of the famous restaurant Lombardi's."

'It was the place where he used to take his wife Julian for a meal."

'He sat down close to the window waiting for the waiter.' He has ordered a big bottle of red wine ."

'It was coming to 7 pm already."

'He thought to himself:' I'm very close to resolving this case. Hm, they have done murder and they think they will get away with it." My poor wife is missing."

'He looked around at the people while he was waiting for the food." he felt very hungry and tired."

'His dinner finally came, was eaten and cleared away."

'Coleman has lit his cigar sitting very comfortable in his chair drinking red wine very slowly."

'He didn't feel to go home that night."

It was a nice jolly atmosphere inside the restaurant."

'He thought about his nice moments spent with his wife Julian."

'Suddenly around 9.30pm his boss Mike turn up with a very attractive dark-haired woman."

'Coleman's eyes opened very wide;' He was trying to hide.'

'He was trying to make sure that Mike won't see him.'

'He moved to another table very close to them so he can observe them."

'He knew that Mike was hiding something.'

'What was caught his eye was the same golden pen."

'The same pen what Coleman has found down the Bronx on the crime scene." This woman was holding the same pen."

'This thing was somehow very important.'

'Coleman was sure now about everything."

'He knew that Mike and this woman were involved in these murders.'

'Coleman's face has turned into the red hot." he felt infuriated."

'He decided to keep calm until he had a result from his friend Andrew."

'They were standing there very close to each other. Her arms were all over him.'

'Mike was enjoying her company. It was obvious.'

'She was looking for a very hot woman in the middle age but very attractive."

'Coleman has thought to himself:" What has happened to Mike was so obvious.'

'At this moment Coleman has hate, Mike.' He couldn't believe with his own eyes."

'He could hear the conversation.' They have been planning to leave the country soon together."

'At that point, Coleman has stood up slowly from the chair and he left the place."

'Luckily he didn't been noticed."

'He sat in the car smoking his cigar.' He decided not to tell Edward what was going on."

He will end this case in his way."

'Driving back home the light of New York City were sparkling as always, especially at night time."

'New York was looking so different at night.' Coleman loved his hometown."

'He came back home very late."

'He sat on his sofa bed holding a glass of brandy.'

'He couldn't believe what he saw in the restaurant. He was suspecting but he had to prove it.'

'Now finally he did put all together in his head."

'Knowing the Mike for a very long time It was hard to believe but people sometimes they do change and that was a case of Mike."

'As he saw the face of the mysterious woman now he can check the criminal record about her. He knew he will have full details about the dark-haired woman."

'Coleman was looking out of the window into the front garden from his bedroom.'

'He lay down on his bed stretching his feet. He took a glass of water from his little table below trying to get some sleep.

'He has to be early in his office."

'As he couldn't sleep he stood up."

'He filled the bathtub and sat in the warm water for about one hour."

'After that, he was ready for the bad."

'The alarm clock wakes him up.' It was at 7 am. He must have slept well for a couple of hours.

'Coleman has put his black trousers and went to the kitchen to make his early morning coffee with some toast."

'He picked up his coffee and drank it off.'

'He was ready to go."

'He locked the door and rush down the stairs."

'Soon after Coleman was on the road driving to his office."

'Finally, he sat down at his chair and he put himself straightaway to work. When someone has knocked on the door."

'Edward came inside holding a couple of files at his hand." he asked;'

'Hey John do you have any news?' His face was very pale.'"Coleman has noticed at first."

'Coleman looked at him then he asked:' Are you ok? You look very pale!'

'Edward murmured:" Oh I think I have got the flu."

'Coleman said:" I think you should go home. I will deal with this case. What are you holding in your hands? John has asked:

Edward took a deep breath:" He responded in a low voice tone." Oh, these are files of l dead bodies we have found so far." I can leave it here with you."

'Coleman has puffed his cigar." He said:" Yes, give it to me. I will take a look later." Go home, Edward. I can manage for today. Call me if you need anything."

Edward said:.' Thanks very much, Coleman." I've appreciated it."

'Coleman has left there on his own." He started to look at woman assassin profile."

'After a couple of hours of research, he finally found her.'

'Her full name was Cecilia Blair."

'She had a long criminal record.." She was working for money."

'Couple of years she was in prison in New Orleans."

'She was known by the name the Black widow."'

'Coleman's eyebrows went up while he was looking at her criminal record."

'He knew he would have to wait for the lab analysis to turn up."

'But there is one more thing what he could do in the meantime."

'He shut the door from his office.'

'He thought to himself:' I have to prove one more thing! I have to prove that Mike's wife didn't die in a car accident."

'He sat in the car. On the way to Mike he bought them lunch and had it in the car."

'Coleman didn't want to waste any more time.'

'He arrived close to Mike's house. He was' Sitting in the car and waiting until Mike has gone out."

'Unfortunately, he didn't have any luck today.' Coleman knew he had to go back tomorrow.'

'Driving back home his brain has been active.'

'He was thinking how all of this will soon end.' He was imagining holding his dear wife Julian in his lovely arms."

'Deep down he knew that his wife is still alive."

'He couldn't understand Mike. Apart from that Mike has been always his good friend."

'How come some people can change so suddenly?" 'Coleman has thought to himself."

'Back to his lovely home, Coleman has taken a glass of brandy."

'He sat comfortably in his chair."

Standing there all alone he felt some sign of deep sadness."

'He couldn't imagine his life without Julian."

'He loved her so much."

'He thought to himself:" I wished I have had at least one child."

'Coleman felt like he was just awakening from the nightmare."

'There was a danger, yes, but this danger was at his workplace."

'Somehow he couldn't relax in his own home anymore, too much stress was in the air."

'He had planned everything for tomorrow morning." He knew he had to go back to Mike's house."

'The important piece of evidence is missing. Coleman has to prove that Mike's wife didn't die in the car accident."

'John has stood up and gone to the kitchen. He made a couple of sandwiches for his

late dinner." He sat down on the sofa bed."

'He picked up his glass of brandy and drank it."

'On the table below were old newspaper he picked them up." he tried to focus his mind on something else."

'He slept on the sofa bed holding the newspaper in one hand."

'The following morning the strong wind has to wake him up.' He must have left the window open in the living room."

'He was feeling very tired.' He dresses quickly."

'It was 7 am." There was a silence in the room." He went to the bathroom, he left the water running from the tap.' He slightly washes his face observing himself in the mirror."

'He thought to himself;" Hmm I need a shave again."

'He poured a big cup of coffee and he sat down to have breakfast."

'Coleman knew his plan for today.' He knew he had to check the car of Mike's wife, he has to get there."

Knowing that Edward was sick at home and Mike wasn't in the office either everything was working well for him."

'He had plenty of time to work out everything."

'Coleman went out of the room he locked the apartment and went out."

'Luckily the Mike House was very close to the Manhattan."

'Coleman was hoping that Mike will go out at some point."

'He already knew the perfect place to park the car, so nobody can see him."

'Coleman was drinking his coffee and puffing the smoke in the air."

'He was waiting until Mike has gone out."

'Something has caught his eye.' Mike was pulling the suitcase, putting the rest of the things in his car.'

'Nicole his daughter has come out." After a couple of minutes, they drove together somewhere."

'Coleman has jumped from the car very quickly, he knew he had the opportunity to check the old car of Mike's wife."

He came closer to the garage trying to pull up the door.' He was struggling."

'He knew he had to be very quick at this point he didn't have much time."

'Turning around all the time to check if somebody was watching him wasn't pleasant at all."

'He knew he was risking a lot."

'After a while, he managed to break the door, he went inside closing the door behind him."

'The old car was there."

'He had to check the brakes on the car."

'He put the light on so he can see properly." He was about to find out when Mike has come back."

'Coleman's face was sweating like hell." He switches the light off and he hides under Mike's wife car."

'He could hear the woman's voice... Coleman knew that must be Cecilia."

'Somehow he wanted to get closer to the door so he could hear the conversation between them."

' 'The door in front of him was connected to the main door. He moves slowly to the main door to hear them better."

'Coleman has heard they been planning the trip together next Friday in Thailand."

'That was a lot to know."

'Nicole Mike's daughter has been sent to her grandparents.'

'Coleman has faced the truth he knew that was all planned."

'He moved again under Mike's wife old car trying to not make any noise."

'He was waiting for hours.' His face was covered in sweat.' lying down in the car on the dirty floor.'

'He was hoping they will go away soon, so he can do this last important thing."

'After a while, Coleman has finally heard them going out.'

"He heard the car was going away.'

'He stood up, he took a deep breath."

'He looked under the car and he did find what he was looking for.' The car brakes were broken on purpose."

'Coleman has taken a photo from the broken car brakes.'

'He finally had nearly all evidence in his hand."

'Coleman has sneaked out from Mike's garage, making sure that everything was left as it was."

'He rushed quickly into his car and he drove off."

'He felt reborn, he felt relieved. He was needing a strong drink after all."

'He decided to go to the 'Old Town Bar.' The place was located at 45 E 18th Street.'

'Coleman thought to himself:' 'there was no doubt now who was in charge of the situation.'

'They were thinking to get away with this but soon all of this It will be over and I will have my wife back."

'Coleman has stopped his car in front of the 'Old Town Bar."

'He steps inside and he orders a glass of brandy."

'He was puffing his cigar."

'He felt tiredness after he had a couple of drinks."

'Coleman has stood there for the last two hours."

'He thought:' I wonder when shall I see my wife Julian."

'He stood up from the chair and he left the Old Town Bar."

'Back at his apartment, he sat on his terrace observing nature."

He thought:" "Peaceful sound, Peaceful place..'"

He said to himself:" You can't go any farther... you've come to the end of things knowing the whole truth."

'Coleman has been waiting for the results to show up."

'He was hoping that his friend Andrew soon he will send him the sooner."

'He has to stop Mike and Cecilia before they run off to Thailand."

'Coleman knew he had one more week left before Mike and Cecilia will leave the country."

'He was needing the results."

'After a couple of days, Coleman received the results. Everything was matching as he thought."

'Edward has just recovered from the flu he had."

'Coleman explain to him what was going on."

'Edward was in shock.'

'Both Detectives have reacted on time.'

'They rushed to the Airport to stop Mike and Cecilia."

'Coleman has informed the Police Force."

'Arriving at the International Airport John.F.Kennedy Coleman was rushing to catch Mike and Cecilia."

'He was looking around and suddenly he saw ."

'He approaches them:" He shouted:" Stop Mike, you are not going anywhere!!!"

'Edward was just behind him."

'Coleman has pointed the gun at his face.."

'Cecilia was in shock, her face had turned pale!'

'Mike said:" What the hell you are doing Coleman." Are you out of mind!!"

'Coleman has puffed the smoke in the air, holding a gun with one hand."

Mike added:" Look here you two..." You make false accusations Coleman."

Coleman said suddenly:" No Mike. Let me finish." You are responsible for those murders Mike." You killed your wife Mike."

'Mike's face has turned into the white his hands were shaking."

He said in a low voice:" I did nothing of the sort."

Coleman shouted:" Shut up Mike." I have got an analysis from the lab." Your wife was cheating on you Mike, she had an affair with a couple of rich men. As you found out she was unfaithful to you.

'You got furious so what did you do, you cat of the car breaks so It was looking like she had a car accident. But It wasn't the car accident you killed your wife Mike."

'Coleman added:" But this is not all Isn't it Mike?

'Soon after that you met Cecilia and we both know that this woman in front of you has a long Criminal Record. Cecilia was in prison in New Orleans for a very long time."

You knew that Mike."

'So you have paid her a lot of money to kill all the men. The lovers from your wife."

Apart from that, you started to have an affair with Assassin woman."

'You have killed Melanie the only witness we have because You were very scared that the real truth will be discovered."

You couldn't risk that much Mike ." Have you? So you killed her.'"

Coleman's eyes were infuriated:" He said:" You also kidnapped my wife."!

'Coleman has pointed with his finger at Mike."

Coleman shouted:" Where is my wife Mike??"

'Mike was shaking, he knew deep down that everything is over."

'Mike has spoken." I'm so sorry Coleman!! Everything that you are saying is real."

'He added:" Your wife is 20 miles from New York close to the 'Erie Canal Village."

'Your wife is there Coleman."

'Coleman took a deep breath." He said:' Make sure my wife is alive, make sure Mike."

'Police were standing there ready to arrest Mike and Cecilia."

'Coleman added:" The last thing Mike."I feel sorry for you." Your jealousy turns you into the worst killer. You have a daughter what you will tell her."

'Coleman has given an order to the Police:" Take them both."

'Coleman has rushed into the car driving fast to rescue his wife."

'Arriving there Julia was lying down on the floor. Her hands were tied up so strong.

'She had bruises all over her body."

Coleman had fallen on the knees, he looked at her face. Her cheeks were coloured with

Emotions."

'She was alive, she was alive.'"

'Ambulance car was on its way.....'

‘

www.ingramcontent.com/pod-product-compliance
Lightning Source LLC
Chambersburg PA
CBHW051905130726
47987CB00002B/985